SLEIGH BELLS in *Park City*

CHRISTMAS IN THE CANYONS * BOOK ONE

HOPE HOLLOWAY

AND

CECELIA SCOTT

Sleigh Bells in Park City

Christmas in the Canyons Book 1

Hope Holloway & Cecelia Scott

Copyright © 2025 Hope Holloway

Christmas in the Canyons

Sleigh Bells in Park City
Snowfall in Park City
Mistletoe in Park City
Midnight in Park City

Chapter One

Cindy

Somehow, Cindy Kessler had made it through Thanksgiving dinner, smiling and talking with family and the few guests they had at Snowberry Lodge this year. She'd held it together during the preparation and baking, the proclamations of gratitude and easy laughter, the dinner and dessert.

Now, wiping a dishtowel over a just-washed roasting pan, she knew it was time to share the very bad news with her sister.

But Cindy just wasn't quite ready to ruin MJ's holiday.

Instead, she absently looked around the sprawling country kitchen, loving this warm, beating heart of Snowberry Lodge. With the scent of cinnamon, roasted turkey, and sweet sage still in the air and the delicate flavor of apple tarts lingering on her tongue, she felt comfortable and secure, and had no desire to take that same feeling away from her dear sister.

They'd both toddled across this wide-planked floor as children. They'd sat at the farmhouse table that their grandfather had made from pine trees that grew on this property. They learned how to cook and bake from their grandmother's wisdom.

Well, MJ had learned how to cook and bake. Cindy had learned how to run a homey, welcoming, and profitable hospitality business.

Regardless of what they'd learned, every inch of Snowberry Lodge was *home*.

Yes, Cindy lived a few miles away in a townhouse now, but she spent the better part of every day here and frequently stayed overnight when the roads were impassible or the work demanded it.

Her sister *did* live here, in the owner's suite off the kitchen. And their father, along with MJ's daughter and grandson, lived at the edge of the property in a mountain home where three generations of Starlings had grown up.

The fact was, Cindy couldn't imagine their family living, working, or gathering anywhere else. And neither could her sister and dearest friend, Mary Jane, known only as MJ since the day she was born.

Right now, MJ stood in front of a long copper sink, humming and wonderfully oblivious to the little bomb about to detonate in her beloved kingdom of cooking.

Not yet. *Not yet.*

As she dried, Cindy's gaze moved to the frosted windows tucked between creamy beadboard cabinets, catching the glimmer of fat snowflakes falling on the pine trees and cabin rooftops.

In the fading evening glow, she could see the rugged terrain of the Wasatch Range in the background, the glorious mountain peaks shrouded in fog.

"Bet some lifts open early this year with this nice powder dump," MJ said, jutting her chin toward the view as she followed Cindy's gaze. "I predict opening day next week instead of early December. And that means an amazing ski season."

Cindy agreed with a nod, looking down at the roasting pan she'd dried four times.

Amazing for who? The Grand Hyatt? All the glitzy new short-term rentals in the mountains, canyons, and all around Park City?

But for Snowberry Lodge? Not so amazing.

Since they were nearing the end of November, Cindy had made the mistake of digging deep into the books she kept as manager of this family-owned business. With their "high season" about to kick off, she hoped their December reservations were not quite as bad as she thought.

They weren't bad—they were worse. That sure took the "thanks" out of Thanksgiving.

It had been a while since they could proudly proclaim "no vacancy" in the eight guest suites in this main lodge or the six cabins that dotted the property. Somehow, they got by.

The ski shop generated decent income through sales and rentals to guests and locals, but this once thriving mountain retreat was...not thriving.

She had to face the truth that she and MJ had hung onto Snowberry Lodge by the skin of their teeth these past few years. And that skin was wearing thin and about to bleed.

"That was an awful heavy sigh for Thanksgiving." MJ eyed her over a large pot she held under the faucet. "Too many apple tarts or are you fretting about something I can talk you out of? 'Cause I will, you know."

She'd certainly try. Her sister had never met a problem she couldn't conquer with an attitude so positive it defied logic.

The fact was, Cindy was a doer, and her older sister was a dreamer. For their whole lives—fifty-nine years for Cindy and sixty-two for MJ—that combination had worked pretty well. But the thing they might have to "do" now could destroy MJ's dreams.

And there was just no good way around it.

"Is there such a thing as too much of anything your daughter bakes?" Cindy asked with a laugh, aching to avoid the conversation and keep things light. "There's a reason she gets a line out the door at Sugarfall."

The compliment brought a glimmer of pride to MJ's sky-blue eyes. She brushed back some hair that had escaped a messy bun, the light catching a few silver threads in the rich auburn.

Cindy expected a comment about her daughter's bakery, but MJ narrowed her gaze to something sharp and questioning. "What is it?" she asked.

"What is...what?"

"Do you forget I can read you like a recipe?" MJ asked. "You've got something on your mind, Cin. Just spill it, okay? This is me. We don't keep secrets."

Cindy closed her eyes. "It's no secret, really. You

know the county changed the tax laws. You know we got reassessed. And you know the bill is due in January."

"Wait. You haven't made monthly payments all year long?" MJ asked.

She shook her head. "We're so stretched, MJ. Payroll, insurance, property management, supplies, and advertising, which we have to do to survive. Everything is expensive. I figured we'd cover taxes with December's profit, since we always have a banner month. But have you looked at the reservations for the next five weeks?"

"Oh, I don't look at those," MJ said with a flick of her sponge. "I plan the menu, get the place decorated, do the shopping, and make every guest feel like family. Oh, that reminds me! I totally forgot to tell you I took a reservation yesterday that you might not have seen."

"The Walker family in Cabin Five? I saw it, counted it, and noticed they didn't have an end date."

"Actually, there's no 'they' or 'family,' at least not as far as I can tell," MJ said. "I talked to the man, and he seemed to be coming alone. But, yes, open-ended and Cabin Five is our most expensive with an unobstructed mountain view. And he did not flinch at our full holiday rate, mind you. Just mentioned he'd pay cash, which I assume you'll take."

"With open hands," Cindy said, grabbing the glimmer of hope. But she couldn't resist adding, "Can you get us about eight more just like that? Fill the cabins and every suite, every day from now until New Year's Day?"

MJ looked at her, a frown pulling as she waited for Cindy to finish.

"And then we might have enough to pay the tax bill." Cindy crinkled her nose. "Emphasis on *might*."

MJ's sweet features fell a little. "Can we talk about it later?" she asked. "Today is Thanksgiving and it's been so nice."

"Of course," Cindy replied. "But we have to—"

"Why do you two always get stuck with cleanup?" Cindy's daughter, Nicole, breezed into the kitchen holding some empty plates, her long dark ponytail swinging with every stride. "Sorry! Gracie and I were caught up in a cousin convo, and I should have known..." Her voice trailed off as she looked from one to the other, letting out a sigh. "Mom. You weren't going to mention it."

No surprise, Nicole could read Cindy as well as MJ. Was she always that transparent or was this particular worry etched on her face?

"I coaxed it out of her," MJ said, rising to Cindy's defense, as she always did. "But now I'm trying to stuff it back like sage dressing in a bird's backside."

Cindy snorted softly.

"Your mother is telling me how lackluster December looks," MJ continued. "I just know reservations will pick up. All over the place families are together right now, having a few drinks, deciding they all need to go to Park City for Christmas. And here we are, waiting with our doors open."

Cindy gave her a dubious look. "We usually have those reservations booked by August or September."

"Well, they're late." MJ waved her Scrub Daddy like it was a magician. "They shall come. You'll see."

Nicole's espresso eyes clouded as she looked at Cindy. "I know you're worried, Mom."

Worried? She'd sailed past worried and slid into panic after looking at those numbers.

"Look, this is a big bill," she said. "Bigger than ever."

"And we have cash on hand," MJ said with certainty.

"If we use it to pay this bill, we won't have anything. No buffer. One leak, one drafty window, one problem and we can't fix it. No ads or special promotions, which are our lifeblood. We're down to the bone, and if we use that money for taxes? The bone's gonna break."

"How did this happen?" MJ asked, concern deepening a faint frown line between her eyes.

Cindy shrugged. "Taxes have gone sky high in Summit County, and we have a *lot* of premium real estate."

"But we're not building on it," MJ said. "The lodge property is mostly woods and hills and slopes and trails. And a creek that's either frozen or flooded."

"That's not how property assessors see it," Cindy told her. "This problem is going to rise up to bite us every December because that bill isn't going anywhere but higher year after year. It's just prohibitively expensive to run a small, family-owned lodge in a resort town like Park City."

MJ stared at her. "What are you saying, Cindy?"

"I'm saying..." She swallowed. "Maybe it would be in our best interest to think seriously about selling Snowberry Lodge."

"*What?*" The question was fired by Gracie, MJ's daughter, as she walked in and froze in shock.

MJ grabbed the edge of the counter and stared at Cindy. "You cannot be serious," she managed to say, then pointed to the dining room behind Gracie. "Benny and Dad can't hear this, can they? Dad would..." She grunted. "His heart couldn't take it."

"They just went into the great room to set up Monopoly by the fire," Gracie assured her, stepping closer to the group as she gathered up some of her hair like the strawberry blond waves were as heavy on her shoulders as this news. "Is it that bad, Aunt Cindy?"

Cindy nodded and put her hand on MJ's back, softening her voice because she knew this was a tough blow.

"Unless something major changes, we'll wipe out our working capital paying this tax bill. We can delay and dance around it, but that means we'll get hit with all kinds of late charges and fees and interest. But if we sold—"

"Stop!" MJ's eyes flashed like gas flames on her beloved old stove. "No one but a Starling has ever owned Snowberry Lodge, or any of the twenty-five acres it sits on," she said on a ragged whisper. "Our married last names might be different, but we are Starlings just the same."

"I know that," Cindy said, staying steady. "But the reason we get taxed from here to kingdom come is because we own some of the most valuable real estate in Utah. In the whole country! But the lodge and cabins are..." She winced, stating the obvious truth. "They just aren't up to the standards of what guests demand these days. Everything needs work and improvements. We could do some over the summer, but we'd need cash that we just don't have."

"But we own Snowberry Lodge free and clear!" MJ exclaimed. "How can there be a money problem?"

She loved MJ more than life itself, but her sister focused on the esoteric aspects of the lodge—food, fun, the atmosphere and decorations. And no one did it better.

MJ didn't really grasp the finances involved in the management of a mountain lodge open for four seasons. The salaries, maintenance, insurance, supplies, overhead, utilities, food and beverage ran many, many thousands a month.

Without full occupancy, they did not make a profit.

Cindy didn't want to utterly wreck Thanksgiving by whipping out a spreadsheet to walk them through the operating budget. "Believe me when I say we're in the deep, deep red. And now we have to pay this astronomical tax bill. I really thought the end-of-year reservations would be higher, but—"

MJ just shook her head, making more hair slip over her cheeks, not hearing one word.

"Snowberry Lodge has been in our family since our grandfather built it more than a hundred years ago, and our girls will inherit it," MJ insisted. "That isn't going to change, Cindy. It can't. I...I don't know how I could ever sleep at night if it did."

"I'm not worried about my inheritance," Nicole said. "But I don't want to give up the ski shed. I've killed myself to build that business."

"I know you have, Nic," Cindy said. Her daughter had turned the ski sales and rental shop at the front of the property into a fine little retail establishment, like Gracie had done with Sugarfall, her bakery in town. "And if we sold, maybe you could keep that business."

"And maybe we could just solve the problem another way," MJ said, crossing her arms. "Nic, you run a fire sale this week. It's Black Friday tomorrow. Let's turn it into 'Get into the Black' Friday. And Gracie?" She turned to her daughter. "Why don't you do a month-long bake-a-thon right here at Snowberry? Or we can run a big promotion for locals that you can advertise in the bakery. And...and...I'll..." She looked from one to the other, her whole face falling as they stared at her, silent. "*Sell?* It's un*think*able, Cin."

Cindy pressed her hand into her sister's narrow, but oh so sturdy, shoulder—the one they all leaned on no matter what was happening.

"I agree with you, and I'm sorry to have to even dance around the idea. But with the Grand Hyatt opening?" Cindy groaned. "We're doomed."

"I hate that word," MJ said.

"Doomed or Hyatt?" Gracie asked dryly.

"Both," MJ scoffed. "Look, we've had thin years before. We always find a way to reinvigorate Snowberry

Lodge. From the day Grandpa Owen brilliantly turned a little horse farm in a mining community into a ski lodge."

"That was the 1960s and he saw the changes coming to Park City," Cindy said.

"And then twenty years later, Dad built the cabins and turned the barn into a gear shed for sales and rentals," MJ continued, undaunted. "That put Snowberry on the map."

Cindy sighed. "The map has changed."

"And then Dad's red hair turned white and the man who'd been called 'Red' his whole life suddenly became the embodiment of Santa Claus, and we were a Christmas destination." She was on a roll now. "And then Jack started the sleigh rides! We literally had a waiting list for this place by June of every year."

"Well, Jack moved to Vermont," Cindy said softly, still hating that particular loss in her life. "So, no one is here to do the sleigh rides and, let's be honest, Red hates being Santa. He won't admit it, but at eighty-two? Our father has had enough with the kids and their demands."

"But he does it," MJ said. "All I'm saying is every single time we've had to, we've reinvented Snowberry Lodge and refused to buckle to change. So, girls..." She looked at Gracie and Nicole. "Let's put on those thinking caps and come up with something."

"Nothing's going to change the situation with the Grand Hyatt," Cindy said, loving MJ's enthusiasm but exasperated with her refusal to face facts. "Deer Valley expanded and that hotel opened right smack dab in the middle of the new lift lines."

"You can see some lifts from here." MJ pointed out to the window.

"But you can't get on one unless you fly," Cindy replied. "And who is going to choose a weathered, dated lodge that requires a van shuttle to the ski resorts? A Grand Hyatt guest can literally grab a gondola to the summit easier than a taxi in the front lobby. And that's *after* you've had a massage at their new spa wing."

"I'll tell you who," MJ said. "People who don't want to pay twenty bucks for a cup of cocoa and don't need a massage and don't mind a nice little shuttle ride. People who like rustic and real, who come to Park City instead of Aspen. I know these people." She gestured to a long open shelf near the mudroom lined with at least a dozen photo albums.

Inside those albums were hundreds of Polaroids of Snowberry's guests, with notes about what they liked and memories of their stay.

"I remember every person who's ever stayed here, and I know something about them, so when they come back, they're family. Do they get that at the Hyatt?"

"They get other things," Gracie said gently, stepping closer to her mother. "Aunt Cindy's right, Mom. Every new customer I have at Sugarfall seems to be staying at the Grand Hyatt. Or one of the five zillion new townhouses or those high-end rentals that came on the market this year."

"We've *always* competed with the big hotels and new builds," MJ insisted, her voice nearly cracking with frustration. "We just need something to bring people back again."

"We need it *now*," Cindy added. "If we could book this place up from now to January and charge top dollar? I could pay the tax bill. But even then, we'll just face the same thing next year."

"Mommy!" Benny shot into the kitchen, bringing the conversation to an abrupt halt. His sweet ten-year-old face was flushed from the sugary dessert, his glasses askew from the excitement of it all. "We've got the Monopoly board set up. Grandpa and I are going to be a team and win!"

"I'm sure you will," Gracie said to her son, who was never far from his beloved great-grandfather. "Nicole and I will be there in one minute and we will not accept defeat!"

"Are you going to play, Grandma?" he asked MJ. "And Aunt Cindy? Then we'd have three teams."

"After we clean up, honey," MJ said. "You play our turns until we get there."

When he left, Gracie leaned in and reached for MJ's hands. "Mom, I promise we'll all put our minds to trying to find a solution. I don't know what I can do from the bakery, but I talk to a lot of people."

"And I'll come up with some way to get more customers in the ski shed and shop," Nicole added. "I know it's a separate business, but it helps Snowberry's bottom line."

"Honey, you're going to be in Vermont," Cindy reminded her.

"I'm not leaving until Saturday, and I won't be gone long. And Aunt MJ mentioned the sleigh rides. If we can't do them, why don't I at least pull the sleigh out of the stables and drape it in lights tomorrow? That'll definitely attract people from the street."

"And freak out poor Copper," Cindy said. "He's never liked that sleigh."

"Because he slid off the trail the very first time Dad and I hitched him to it," Nicole said. "But without Jack Kessler, no one's giving sleigh rides."

At the second mention of her ex-husband and Nicole's father, Cindy gave a sad smile. Certainly no one was giving rides the way he had—with style, grace, and a full Victorian Christmas caroler costume.

She covered the moment of sadness by waving Nicole and Gracie out of the kitchen. "Go play Monopoly, and don't let those two win. And you're right," she said. "We'll think of ideas and not give up yet."

"Let us help you clean up," Gracie said, but MJ nudged her away.

"Don't mess with tradition," she said. "Aunt Cindy and I have been the Thanksgiving clean-up crew for fifty years." She added a playful look at Cindy. "And if I have my way, we'll be the clean-up crew for...a few more. Not fifty, but a few."

The girls smiled and blew kisses, heading to the main gathering room at the front of the lodge, where Cindy knew the fire was crackling and the snow could be seen out all the windows.

After a beat, Cindy went back to drying a pan and

MJ reached for a crystal wine glass. As she rinsed the stemmed goblet, she exhaled.

"These were Grandma Irene's," she said, holding up the cut glass to the light. "They've been in the Starling family forever."

Cindy didn't respond because she knew it was MJ getting sentimental over the memories of family, Christmases, and guests that had filled this three-story inn for so many decades.

"You're serious about this, aren't you?" MJ finally asked.

"I'm scared to death about it, too," Cindy said. "I know you think I'm just being my pragmatic self but—"

Still holding the glass, MJ put an arm around her. "Little sister, didn't I just remind you that I know what's going on in that head of yours? I've known you since Mom brought you home and presented me, a three-year-old, with my own living, breathing baby doll."

Cindy smiled, knowing the story well, but never tiring of it.

"I shared a bedroom with you for more than twenty years. I have cooked in this kitchen while you ran the lodge since Dad retired. I held your hand through a painful divorce, and you held mine when George died far too young, and we cried together when Mama passed. I know what you're thinking and what you're feeling. I know you try to be practical and mathematical and all businessy, just like I know it hurts you the same as it hurts me. I can see it all over your pretty face."

Cindy felt that face nearly crumple with tears, overcome with love for this woman.

"I'm so sorry to ruin your Thanksgiving," she whispered.

MJ squeezed her eyes as if the words sliced her in half. "I refuse to give up." She ground out the words. "The Snowberry Lodge is a landmark and a legacy. I will not give up yet."

"MJ, you have to look at the numbers. This place is worth a literal fortune."

"And you have to look at the history!" she exclaimed. "Yes, I know the value of twenty-five acres on the outskirts of Park City, Utah. But what price can you put on the blood, sweat, and tears shed by every Starling since Grandpa Owen and Grandma Irene lived and died here? What's that worth, huh?"

Millions, Cindy thought glumly. A bunch of them.

"We'll climb out of this hole," MJ said, lifting her chin with confidence. "Do I know how? No, I do not. But I'm not ready to roll over and...*sell*."

She practically spat the word that was so deeply distasteful to her.

"You see history and family, MJ," Cindy said quietly. "But the guests who pay to stay here see a relic from years gone by. They see outdated furniture, ancient finishings, long treks in a shuttle and drafty cabins and...no spa."

"We can upgrade the bathrooms, and I bet new insulation would fix the drafts."

Remodeled bathrooms wouldn't put this place on a

lift line, Cindy knew. And an equity loan would saddle them with back-breaking debt.

She leaned into her sister. "I'm sorry I brought this up on Thanksgiving, MJ. I know you love the holidays so much."

"But you hate them."

"No! I don't hate them," she said, then laughed guiltily. "I'm not exactly...Mrs. Claus, but I don't hate them. It's just...never easy."

She didn't want to say why, and with MJ? She didn't have to. Her sister knew the history and, as she'd just mentioned, she'd held Cindy's hand ten years ago when Jack Kessler left on Christmas Day, moved to Vermont, and chose his career over her.

MJ gave a sympathetic look that softened every feature on a face Cindy loved. "I know, hon. And when Nic goes to see him, that's hard."

"I like that they try to stay close," she said. "I don't mind that she goes to Vermont. I understand she misses him. I...do, too, sometimes." The admission caught in her throat, and she covered it with a tight smile.

"We all miss him," MJ said. "He broke my heart when he left you, but I loved that guy and all his...Jackness. All that energy and positivity." She walked over to the old glass-front hutch painted in a weathered sage, reaching for a door. "He'd know how to fix this problem," she said, so softly Cindy almost didn't hear her over the creak the hutch made when she opened it.

"Well, he's not here," Cindy said, adopting her most

rational tone, the one that usually quieted MJ's silly dreams. "And we have to solve the problem ourselves."

"Not by selling."

"It's extreme, I know, but the money we'd get would set our girls up for life. And we could retire."

MJ snorted. "And do what?"

"I don't know. Test out that new spa at the Grand Hyatt."

"I'd rather drown in a hot tub," MJ said. "And our girls are just fine. They're brilliant businesswomen, both of them. Who's smarter than Nicole and Gracie?"

"Benny," Cindy said on a laugh. "Your grandson is a genius, you know that?"

"Oh, I know. That boy is a brainiac, isn't he?"

"Well, if his brain could figure out how to fill the reservation book in December, I'd get him that puppy he wants myself."

"Gracie's not so sure she wants that commitment."

"She'd rather live here with a puppy than somewhere else without one, right?" Cindy challenged. "And if we don't fill this place between now and January first, we might be selling and moving."

"We are not—"

Cindy looked up when MJ didn't finish, following her sister's gaze to the hall.

"Was that Benny?" MJ whispered.

Cindy's chest sank a little. "I hope not. He shouldn't hear any of this."

"I'll go check on him," MJ said, drying her hands on a dish towel.

They exchanged a glance—equal parts dread and affection for the boy they both adored—then MJ disappeared through the arched doorway.

Cindy turned to eye the mountains again, smiling at the snowfall. This was definitely what her ex-husband would call a great, big glorious powder dump.

Nothing made Flying Jack Kessler happier than a few feet of fluffy, ski-perfect snow on his beloved slopes.

She closed her eyes and willed the memory away.

Jack was a long-closed chapter of her life, and she couldn't ever hear that laugh again any more than she could fill this place to the rafters and save Snowberry Lodge.

But MJ was right with all her ruthless optimism. They had to try. They had to.

Chapter Two
Nicole

Nicole Kessler trudged up the path from the street-facing parking lot to reach the ski shed the morning after Thanksgiving, her boots sinking into snowdrifts as she forged her way to work.

Almost there, she took a moment to notice the Utah mountain skies were heartbreakingly blue around the ridgeline, freshly washed from the storm. That sight would bring joy to all the avid skiers about to descend on Park City for the start of the season.

Nicole could speak their language, and she would, all day today, when skiers came into the Snowberry Lodge Adventure Shack—AKA the ski shed—to buy and rent everything they'd need to hit the slopes.

But speaking their language didn't make her one of them. Yes, she catered to ski lovers all winter long, who chatted endlessly about the conditions, the runs, the lines, the crowded slopes, the cost of lift tickets. But she hadn't put on a pair of boots and bindings for... what?

Nineteen years.

Well, eighteen years and ten months, to be precise. January would be the nineteenth anniversary of her accident, and she still couldn't imagine what it would take to get her on the slopes again.

She kept her history well hidden from her customers, and with what was going on at the lodge? The worry in her mother's eyes and the agony in Aunt MJ's? She'd faked the ski love with every person on the property because Nicole's little piece of the Snowberry pie was helping to keep this place afloat.

Digging into her bag for the keys, she studied the building, which wasn't actually a shed at all. Situated about fifty yards across a wide drive from the main lodge, the shop was a converted barn painted bright red with a dark green tin roof and a massive display window. Behind the glass was an ever-changing array of ski apparel, boots, helmets, and gleaming skis and poles.

A sign for the shed at the street entrance to Snowberry Lodge invited locals and tourists to buy and rent anything they'd need for the slopes in the winter, plus bikes and hiking gear in the summer. Here, they'd pay much less than they would at the resorts or even in town.

Off to the right, a carport housed the lodge's shuttle van and a muddy UTV that Nicole loved to take through the trails in the warmer weather. The van was gone now since Brianna Larsson, her roommate, co-worker, and bestie, was at the airport picking up some new arrivals.

Unlocking the oversized front door, she walked into her spacious, high-ceilinged shop, its open floor ringed by a railed loft where all the skis stood like colorful soldiers.

On the main floor, racks of apparel, shelves of accessories, and displays of gear filled the warm, well-lit space.

With undeniable pride, Nicole scanned the store and her merchandise, satisfied that everything was arranged to catch the sun that poured through the high windows around the second-floor loft.

Nicole might hate skiing—with a passion—but adored her little retail paradise. Since she'd turned fifteen, she'd worked at the ski shed, helping Grandpa Red run this end of Snowberry's business.

All the way through high school and four years at the University of Utah, Nicole worked here every holiday and summer, slowly but surely putting her touch on the place.

As a business major with a minor in retail management, taking over the ski shed had been a natural move, and Grandpa Red had been more than happy to retire at seventy-five.

For the past seven years, Nicole had expanded the merchandise, improved the displays, and launched some successful ad campaigns.

She also hired Brianna, her closest friend from college and an avid skier, to help with lessons when she started that business. Brianna had brought a new energy and excitement, and had taken over running the shuttle service, too.

She loved this job so much that she couldn't bear to think about the kitchen conversation last night. Sell Snowberry? She groaned at the very idea, vowing to somehow slay her own sales numbers and be able to help with that tax bill.

But first...Copper. With an hour before opening the

shop's doors, she grabbed her jacket again and headed outside to the stable, a minute's walk from the shed.

Pushing open the heavy wooden door, the warm scent of hay and horse wrapped around her, a sharp contrast to the crisp morning air still clinging to her cheeks. Inside, Copper nickered low from his stall, already shifting his weight in anticipation.

"There's my boy," she murmured, crossing the straw-covered floor. He stuck his head over the stall door, his reddish coat dusted with bits of hay, nostrils flaring to greet her.

She ran a hand down the white streak on his long, warm face, getting a push of love when she reached into her pocket for the peppermint he fully expected her to have.

Mom and Dad had given this horse to Nicole for her high school graduation, after Whistler had gone to the great stables in the sky. She always thought Copper was some kind of consolation prize for her parents' divorce, which happened later that same year during her freshman fall semester at the University of Utah.

Maybe they'd hoped to ease her pain with this beautiful beast.

Of course, Snowberry Lodge always had a horse or two, and they always had someone on staff who acted as a stable manager when Nicole was at school or work. But there were few things she treasured more than being able to get over here early to feed, brush, exercise, and warm her big boy.

He was fourteen now, a beautiful Belgian Draft horse

with a sturdy build and feathered legs. A gentle giant except for when he got spooked, Copper sported a reddish-chestnut coat and a light flaxen mane. His striking winter look was perfectly photogenic for the sleigh he was purchased to pull.

Except he hated getting hitched to the darn thing as much as Nicole hated sliding into a pair of skis. So, she'd get him outside for exercise before she got that sleigh out of storage.

She did all the stable chores first, then took him out to the paddock after refilling his water and tossing a few flakes of hay into his feeder. While he wandered around and got some air, she went back inside to a massive tack and storage area, throwing off the big blanket that covered the sleigh nestled in a corner.

Letting out a low whistle, she took a good look at the iconic piece of Snowberry history.

Good heavens, it was beautiful. A classic open carriage, it had a deep cherry red body with two rows of black leather seating for as many as six people. The front was open, adding a true measure of glory for the driver, while the spacious back seat was tucked low and flanked by lanterns and warmed with red blankets.

Oh, yes, this had marketing potential, even at a standstill.

She could pile the front seat high with some fake Christmas presents, string lights all over it, and let the kids ring the sleigh bells.

That would help draw customers, if only for the social media-worthy Christmas photos.

She wandered around the beast, trying to figure out how to pull it out, climbing over some saddles, piles of harnesses, and a wooden ramp she remembered that Grandpa Red made for a handicapped guest who used to visit every year and liked to sit on Whistler.

Grabbing hold of the sleigh, she managed to push it toward the doors, stopping as she got to the entrance to gather up her strength.

"Nicole!" Benny came darting down the hill from the house where he lived with Gracie and Grandpa, his down jacket wide open, his hat about to fly off his never-combed hair. "Are you going on a sleigh ride? Can I come? Please?"

"Hey, little cuz," she called, waving him over. "No ride, but I need your muscles."

"I don't have muscles," he said as he trudged through the snow. "And I'm technically your first cousin once removed. Although I don't know what it's removed *from*."

She snorted a laugh at the family genius, loving her cousin's son like a baby brother, no matter the technicalities of their bloodline. "You have enough muscles for this. I just need a little push onto the driveway. Once we're there, it'll slide easily enough."

"What's it for?"

"Decoration."

"Why?" he asked, bracing himself next to her. Always, *always* asking why, this kid.

"To attract customers. Push."

"So, we don't have to...move?" he grunted on the last word.

She froze, looking down at his childish features and the frosted glasses he'd worn since he was three. "What?"

"I heard Aunt Cindy and Grandma MJ talking last night. Aunt Cindy wants to move."

"No, she doesn't, and you shouldn't worry about stuff like that, kiddo. Adults will handle it."

"But Grandma MJ said we should put our thinking caps on." He touched the green knit beanie on his head. "Great-grandpa Red says I'm a *human* thinking cap. I can help."

She wanted to laugh, but her heart tightened at the thought of this little sweetie worrying about things like that. "Yes, you probably can. But I want you to promise me something."

He gave the sleigh a decent shove. "What?'"

"All you are going to think about from now until Christmas is...well, Christmas. You know, presents and decorations and carols and presents and...did I mention presents?"

He gave her that "wise beyond his years" expression he wore so well. "Christmas isn't just about presents," he said, so serious she had to bite her lip to keep from chuckling. "I want to help with...the not moving thing."

"Oh, Benny." She took her hands off the sleigh to hug him. "You're so awesome. And you know how you can help? Decorate this sleigh for me. Just get some empty boxes and wrap them in Christmas paper and then find a few sets of extra lights and drape them all over. Could you do that?"

"Of course!" he exclaimed. "It's like I have a mission!"

"Operation Sleigh Bells," she teased.

Practically vibrating with excitement, Benny helped her with the sleigh, the two of them getting it nicely situated outside the ski shed. He took off to accomplish his mission just as she spotted some customers pulling into the lot.

"I'll be right with you!" she called, then hustled to get Copper blanketed and back inside. As she guided him into the stables, the big horse slowed at the sight of the sleigh, neighing noisily and kicking one of his white-stockinged legs.

"Still your nemesis, eh?" Nicole teased, giving his mane a rub. "No worries, big guy. It's just there for decoration. Kind of like you."

Business was steady all morning, but during a break in the flow, she heard the motor of the shuttle van, some voices outside, and then Brianna's boots in the back office.

"Hey, Nic," Brianna called. "How are our Black Friday sales?"

"Dark gray," she replied, turning to see her closest friend step into the store, unzipping her puffer jacket.

Brianna's long, nearly platinum blonde hair tumbled out from a knit headband, her hazel eyes sparking with joy. "What is that sleigh doing out there?"

"Waiting for lights," Nicole said. "I thought it might bring in customers."

"Always the marketing queen," her friend quipped. "You know what else will attract customers? All that glorious, beautiful, white, fluffy, dusty, delicious pow-*der*. Woot!"

Nicole laughed at that, expecting nothing less from this snow bunny.

The daughter of Swedish immigrants who'd moved to the Salt Lake area when Bri was a baby, she lived for a good black diamond run on a day as sunny as her personality.

Nicole met Brianna Larsson their freshman year at the University of Utah and the two of them had stuck together ever since. Over their college years, Brianna had come to Snowberry Lodge many times and fell in love with the place.

Since then, they'd shared several apartments and now a townhouse twenty minutes away.

"How were the new guests?" Nicole asked as she headed toward the pole wall to straighten one a customer had moved.

"Guest," she corrected. "Just one old guy all alone."

"That's weird." Nicole kneeled on the display and reached up, fiddling with the pole. "Is this straight?"

"It's fine. You're a perfectionist." Brianna pulled some drawers behind the register. "Where are my gummy worms?"

"In the trash, where they belong."

"Say it ain't so."

"It ain't. Top drawer, on the right." Nicole climbed down and started on the boots. "Who comes to a resort alone?"

"Same weirdo who pays cash," she said over the

rustle of her candy bag. "I don't care how old you are—use a credit card or Venmo, for crying out loud."

"How old was...What was his name?"

"Mr. Walker. And he might need one—a walker, I mean. He's gotta be...sixty-five."

Nicole snorted. "Don't let my Aunt MJ or my mother hear you call that old."

Brianna came around the counter, digging into her candy bag. "You ready for Vermont?" she asked. "Three days with The Legend!" She wiggled a candy worm. "You know I never get enough stories of Flying Jack Kessler."

Nicole rolled her eyes, long used to Brianna being starstruck over Dad's impressive ski resume and reputation. "All he's going to do is try to put skis on me. The winter visits are always the hardest."

"I say face your fears, Miss Kessler, and let your father—a two-time Olympic competitor who won silver in the FIS Alpine Ski World Cup—teach you how to ski again. He's Jack Kessler. I mean, come on. I came of age listening to him doing color commentary for every Alpine event I ever watched."

As a wannabe-but-never-was championship skier, Brianna knew the sport inside and out.

"And I came of age with him jetting off to Vancouver or Sochi or wherever ESPN sent him. Honestly, you probably know his voice better than I do."

Brianna angled her head. "You're usually happy to see him, Nic. What's wrong?"

"We have big problems at Snowberry," she said, not

bothering to sugarcoat it with her closest friend, and easily admitting what was on her heart. "A fat tax bill is due, and we do not have the cash to cover it. We'll have to be late, pay fees, and it'll be even more next year. My mom thinks it might be smart to sell the whole place."

Brianna abandoned the candy bag, tossing it on the counter to step closer. "Nic! I knew business was slow and that the new resorts have eaten into bookings, but... wow. Really? Sell? How can you? This place has been in your family since Park City was founded."

"Not quite, but darn near," she agreed. "Short term, we have to build the business over the holidays, which are usually our boom time. If we could, Mom can cover the tax bill. But long term?" She huffed a breath. "I don't know. This place is worth a lot of money and selling it would be...easier."

"And awful," Brianna said.

"I've added a ton of inventory to our sale, because we're all trying to come up with some kind of miracle to save December's numbers."

Brianna stared at her, narrowing eyes that cut right down the middle between green and brown. Slowly, she nodded, then started snapping her fingers as an idea hatched. "You know what you should do?" she asked, pointing a finger at Nicole. "Get your dad here."

Nicole drew back. "Are you high on gummy worms?"

"I'm serious."

"What good would that do?"

"He was the sleigh ride king of the mountain," she

said. "I've heard the stories. Everyone wanted to ride with Flying Jack."

"The stories are true," Nicole said, grabbing so many old memories from her childhood. "Dad ran that sleigh so fast, it was a wonder he *didn't* fly. And with Red all dressed up like Santa? They were the Snowberry glory days. Whistler loved it. But Copper?" She made a face. "He slipped off the trail on his first ride the same Christmas my dad moved away. Trauma all around and the sleigh's been still ever since."

Brianna lifted a brow. "I'm telling you. Get your dad to bring his Hallmark movie magic back to this place. That'll help bookings and I assume the rides aren't free."

"They cost a pretty penny and are worth it," Nicole agreed. "And it would help reservations to run that sleigh. Other resorts might have spas and lift access, but no one has sleigh rides."

"The ultimate winter adventure fantasy and Instagram perfection," Brianna said. "Get Jack to come back for one month and give sleigh rides, Nic."

If only it were that easy. "He's not coming back. You know the history of him and my mom."

"I remember when you were dealing with the divorce freshmen year," she said. "We had some tough conversations in the dorm lounge."

Oh, they had. They'd been next-door neighbors in Chapel Glen, their freshman dorm, but their roommates were both pretty weird, so Brianna and Nicole bonded immediately. They'd shared many personal stories, including the heartache of Nicole's parents' split.

"Then you remember that Mom filed for divorce because she thought it would be a drastic enough move to get him to retire from ESPN, which she not so lovingly called 'the other woman.'" Nicole huffed out a breath at the memory. "But he wouldn't retire, and, in true Flying Jack form, he actually left on Christmas so he could *fly* to a time trial for Men's Super-G."

"Well, that was his signature race," Brianna said. "Not that it forgives a Christmas departure."

"Well, I've forgiven him," Nicole said. "Just like he's forgiven me for quitting skiing."

"That's a little different," Brianna said. "You darn near died at nine years old."

Nicole just shook her head, never a fan of the subject of her accident. "Anyway, my parents split up and...that's that," she said.

"But is that truly *that*?" Brianna challenged.

"Yes, it is. He went to Vermont because his parents retired there. Why would he come back here?"

"How many times have you caught your mom looking through old pictures or watching tapes from your childhood or their wedding video?" Brianna challenged.

"One time." Nicole made a face, remembering the evening about a year ago, when she'd walked in on her mother doing just that. "Yeah, I think she regrets the divorce."

"And so does he," Brianna said.

"You've met the man once."

"Twice," she corrected, flipping back her fat blond braid. "I met him at graduation and another time when I went to Stowe with a ski club, remember? You arranged for me to have dinner with him."

"And you asked him a million questions about being in the Olympics," Nicole recalled. "He loves talking about his glory days."

"And his life. After all, he's my bestie's dad, so I was interested. When he talked about Cindy...well, I swear I could see a little sadness in his eyes."

"I don't know," Nicole said, her heart tightening at the thought of her parents still loving each other.

Brianna pointed at her. "One month, Nic. Surely he'd do that for you and his...his ex-family at Snowberry."

She searched her friend's face, thinking hard about the possibility. They had all promised to do whatever they could to help. Was *this* the idea that might actually work? Dad back at Snowberry on the sleigh?

She turned as the front door opened. "Customers," she whispered. "Let's focus on something that *will* make us money."

"You know it could work, Nic."

It could. But Dad coming back to Park City was about as likely as her barreling down a black diamond run. "Great idea, Bri, but it's not happening. Let's drop it."

The family of four needed two sets of skis, poles, boots, and their little girl wanted to buy a North Face jacket—and they were on sale as of a few hours ago, so the mom got one, too.

The minute the shoppers left—after racking up a

lovely four-figure receipt—Brianna slid next to Nicole at the cash register.

"I can't," Brianna confessed.

"You can't what?"

"Drop it."

Nicole exhaled a laugh. "Well, you're wasting your time."

"He's retired, right? Not doing color commentary anymore?" she pressed. "What does he have to do over the holidays?"

She had no idea what a sixty-year-old former ski champion did with his free time now that he was done with broadcast television "Ski, I imagine, if the Stowe lifts are working and there's snow."

"He could ski here. We don't call it 'the greatest snow on Earth' for nuthin'."

"True," Nicole agreed. Few things thrilled her dad more than skiing in Utah.

Born and raised right here in Park City, Jack Kessler had grown up bombing down these slopes, joining the junior racing circuit as a kid. By sixteen, he'd had a spot on the U.S. Ski Team development roster and a reputation as a local idol. As an adult, he competed all over the world, including two times at the Olympics, though he never medaled.

An injury sidelined his career and a holiday job interview at Snowberry introduced him to the woman he'd marry.

What would it take for him to come back?

"Go get him," Brianna insisted on a whisper, as if she

could follow Nicole's train of thought. "Lure him to Park City with promises of hot cocoa and a horse-drawn sleigh —and the best skiing in the country. He could be a hero, save the lodge, and have the Christmas of his dreams."

She stared at her friend, hating that the idea actually...could work.

"But my mother..."

"Please." Brianna scoffed. "Shove those two under some mistletoe and let the sparks fly."

Nicole gasped, the thought was so...*enchanting.* Perfect, even. "What a dream that would be, Bri. I mean, they were happy once. Before Dad started traveling so much for his big TV job. Before skiing stole him away again."

The ache settled into her chest like it always did when she thought about it for too long.

"They should never have gotten divorced," Brianna said. "I mean, I don't know the whole history, but it just never made sense to me."

"Or me," Nicole said glumly. "He loved us. He *still* loves us. But skiing was his identity. After his injury, he felt like he lost himself. The sleigh rides helped, I think. And he did so much for Snowberry Lodge. But when ESPN came calling, it was like he finally saw a way back to that world."

"And your mom couldn't compete with it," Brianna finished softly.

Nicole shrugged. "They tried. But it always felt like he was chasing something more, like the lodge—and us— weren't enough for him. Mom was too busy to ski much and I wouldn't go, so he jumped at the ESPN gig. All they wanted him to do was travel and he was never home, and she wanted him to quit. He wouldn't. And now ten years have passed."

Brianna gave her a look. "Ten years is enough for them to forget what broke them but still feel what brought them together. You can ask, right? What do you have to lose?"

"He'll say no," she said, already certain.

But that didn't stop her from imagining...the unimaginable. Mom and Dad. Sleigh rides and mistletoe.

Now *that* could be the miracle the Snowberry Lodge needed.

Chapter Three
Red

"Grandpa! Great-grandpa!" Something poked his cheek. Then again. A finger—definitely a finger. "Benedict Starling!"

Who was that? No one called him Benedict, not since he was knee high to a—

"Hey, Red! Wake up unless you're dead, then gimme your phone so I can call 911."

He opened one eye, then the other, pulled from the comfort of his BarcaLounger to peer up into the far-too-close face of his ten-year-old great-grandson.

Really, the only human who could wake Red Starling from a noon-time nap and live to tell the tale.

"Benny," he growled, scrubbing a hand over his face. "What in the name of—"

"You said you were watching me, remember?" Benny reminded him, chipper as a chipmunk. "Only you weren't, because you fell asleep with the TV on and your mouth open like this." Benny mimicked a cartoon snore and flopped his head back dramatically.

Red raised the recliner with a grunt. "I wasn't asleep. I was...resting my eyes."

"For an hour," Benny said. "I timed it."

"'Course you did." Red squinted at the clock on the mantle. He had meant to rest for fifteen minutes. Maybe twenty. Darn turkey leftovers.

"Well..." He groaned, hauling himself upright while every joint in his body filed a formal complaint. "You're still breathing and not on fire, so I'd say I did a fine job."

Benny grinned. "I need help with something important. I tried to do it all myself, but some jobs only the great Santa Starling can manage."

Oh, boy, he was layin' it on thick now. "Like what?"

"It's a decorating emergency," Benny said. "Come on, I'll show you."

Red followed the boy out of the living room, stepping carefully over a pile of ribbons and wrapping paper, and into the den. What awaited him looked like a Christmas explosion gone sideways.

"What fresh headache is this?" he muttered, taking in the tangled mess of string lights, half-emptied boxes marked "Christmas decs" in MJ's handwriting, and a pile of ornaments haphazardly dumped on the coffee table.

Benny stood in the center of it all like a commander on a battlefield. "I'm decorating the sleigh Nicole dragged out of storage."

"The sleigh? Who's gonna drive that thing? If you say 'Santa,' then you *will* be on fire or not breathing."

"No one is driving it. Nicole has to put it out front to attract people."

Red felt his face form a scowl. "People. Who wants them?"

"Aunt Cindy and Grandma MJ!" he exclaimed.

"'Cause if we don't have more people, we're going to move! To another house! Not Snowberry Lodge. Can you imagine that, Grandpa?"

Now that was the most ridiculous thing he ever heard. He'd been born on this land, and he'd die here. He'd lived in this very house, a two-story timber-framed family home near the edge of the property, from birth to... that last nap.

His pa, Owen Starling, had built this as the family house on the property when he had the foresight to turn the original residence into Snowberry Lodge.

With its pitched metal roof, wide covered porch, and weathered cedar siding, Starling House, as it was known, had a quiet sturdiness that came from decades of lived-in love.

Red rubbed the back of his neck, a slow, dark worry crawling up his chest. They liked to keep things from him, those daughters of his. Didn't want to worry him. Never wanted to stress his old heart.

What was this all about? Were they going to move the three of them into some kind of cookie-cutter condo and try to rent this place for extra money?

"What in the world does a sleigh have to do with that?" he asked, sensing that his great-grandson—the single smartest whip Red had ever met—knew more than he was letting on.

Benny's face grew serious, but then this was Benny. Serious was his middle name—along with internet, apps, and all that other stuff that made Red's teeth itch.

"I heard Aunt Cindy last night. She was talking to

Grandma MJ and said something about selling Snowberry. Said we might have to close the lodge. And then we'd all have to move."

Selling...Snowberry Lodge? The floor dropped out from under Red's stomach, and he reached for the doorjamb to steady himself. "What?"

"So, Nicole said we need to decorate the sleigh." He lifted a snarled mess of lights. "We have to, Grandpa!"

"No need to sound desperate."

"I am desperate, because get this!" He danced on his toes as if he couldn't contain himself. "If we get enough business, Aunt Cindy is going to get me a puppy!"

Red drew back. "Your mama know that?"

"Aunt Cindy said she didn't care," he said confidently. "So we have to decorate the sleigh and get people here. Don't you see, Grandpa?"

He couldn't see anything but...selling Snowberry? He'd do anything to stop that. Anything.

"And this looks like something you'd be really good at," he prattled on, handing him a nest of Christmas lights. "I borrowed your phone while you were snoring and asked the AI app, but it didn't help me untangle Christmas lights."

He groaned. That dang phone. He hated everything about it and gave it to Benny whenever he needed something. Gracie didn't like that, though. She had a hard and fast "no phone" rule for the boy, which Red tried to respect but, dang, sometimes he needed Benny's help to work that stinking device.

Red held up the knotted lights. "God himself doesn't know how to untangle these beasts."

"You can do it, Grandpa," Benny said. "You're Red Starling. You can do anything."

Red felt a smile pull as he looked down at the kid, not sure if that was a crock of hooey or hero worship. Either way, he fell for it.

"I'm going to wrap the fake presents," Benny announced, pulling out a roll of...was that duct tape?

With a ragged sigh, Red looked at the lights, the mess of boxes, but his focus fell on the old fur jacket lying across the ottoman like a lazy dog. Oh, the Santa outfit he climbed into every blasted year because he had the good fortune to be fat, bald, and sport a six-inch beard that had turned whiter than the snow that fell last night.

That jacket, that role—the whole month, to be honest —was the bane of Red's existence. He was so darn sick of ho-ho-hoing those little greedy bra...kids.

But if things at the lodge were that bad? Well, yeah. Red didn't shy away from his responsibilities. That didn't mean he liked them, though.

Stepping into the mess, he grabbed the jacket and slipped it on, smelling the musk of the attic mixed with the lingering scent of peppermint and pine.

"It still fits." He pulled the front around his belly and tugged at the slight gap. "Almost." *Oh, Gracie.* Why did his granddaughter have to own the best bakery in Park City and bring her leftovers to him?

Benny made a face. "The belt will hold it together."

Red chuckled despite himself and let the jacket hang

open. "All right. What do you need me to do? Let's make it fast..." He picked up the old Santa hat and pulled it on his bald head. "'Fore I turn you into an elf."

Benny giggled and slapped some gray tape on a very badly wrapped box. They worked in a companionable silence for a bit, then headed out for phase two of what Benny called his "special mission."

He was certain that decorating a useless sleigh would somehow translate into a puppy his mother didn't want to add to her long list of responsibilities. And Red could see that the sleigh might attract customers, which were apparently in very short supply.

Outside, the snow had stopped falling but the yard still sparkled with a fresh coat of white powder, clean and pristine under the late afternoon light. The sleigh—old, red, and charmingly beat-up—had been dragged to a nice spot in front of the ski shed.

It wasn't shiny and all decked out, but it looked better than Red for its age—and they were probably about the same eighty-two years old. That thing had been around Snowberry Lodge for as long as he could remember.

With the Santa jacket providing the only warmth he needed, he hoisted up some wrapped packages on to the seats. Yeah, they looked like the entire elf crew had been inebriated while they worked. But it was festive enough.

After that, he and Benny started threading string lights along the sides of the sleigh. Red's arthritic fingers weren't much help with the tiny plastic clips, but he did what he could.

"Careful with those cords," he warned the boy. "Last

time I got zapped, I smelled like burnt chestnuts for a week."

"It's not even plugged in," Benny said. "And these are LEDs. They barely get warm. Plus, I can put an app on your phone so you can turn them on and off right from your recliner."

"Please don't," he said.

After twenty minutes of grumbling, laughing, and Benny stringing extension cords like he had an electrician's license, the sleigh sparkled with twinkle lights, candy cane ribbons, and pretend presents.

Two massive gold bells, meant for the horse, hung from the front with a wreath Benny had "borrowed" from one of the cabin doors.

"There." Benny clapped his hands. "Now you have to sit in it."

"Why?"

"Because I want a picture." He waved Red's phone, which spent a lot more time in Benny's hands than his own. "You're Santa. Come on, just for one picture."

He didn't like it, but he climbed into the front, lifting the reins.

"I wish we could get Copper," Benny said.

"He'd just fuss," Red replied, easing into the seat. "That horse never liked the sleigh." The leather was cold and stiff, not comfortable at all. He slouched, stretched his legs, and tugged the hat lower over his eyes.

"Can I nap now?"

Benny held up his phone. "Say cheese, Santa."

Red scowled and Benny giggled.

"You look mad."

"I am mad. I was born mad, and this dang itchy jacket makes me madder. You're lucky I like you, son."

Benny kept fiddling with the phone. "Okay, keep talking like that. Say something like Santa would."

"Like what?"

"I don't know. Something Christmasy. Pretend you're doing a commercial for the Snowberry Lodge that would get people to come here."

Red groaned. "I don't like people," he said dryly.

"Grandpa!"

"Okay, okay." He sat up straighter. "Merry whatever you want to call it. Come spend money at the Snowberry Lodge. We got ski stuff, good food, pretty views, and a sleigh that probably won't collapse under your mother-in-law. No promises, though. Ho ho ho *no*."

Benny burst out laughing. Then, still snickering, he tapped something on his phone. "I'm making you an account."

"Like at a bank?"

"I'm calling it Grumpy Santa. It's a TikTok. And Instagram. Just for fun. I bet people would love you."

"Your mother won't like that."

"Then it'll be our secret, as you like to say." Benny grinned as his little fingers flicked over that screen like he was playing an instrument.

Gracie might do her level best to keep technology out of those ten-year-old hands, but Red knew it was a losing battle. The kid was a prodigy and Red loved him more than he loved Gracie's creampuffs.

They spent more time outside, the mid-day sun making it bearable. They added a garland to the nearby pine tree, adjusted light strands, and positioned the sleigh just so.

Through it all, Benny had that phone out, and Red got into the Grumpy Santa bit. How could he not? Benny egged him on, and it was admittedly kind of fun.

He even let Benny drape an old jingle bell collar around his shoulders for effect.

The cold air bit at Red's cheeks, but the sight of Benny's joy—the way he danced back and forth, checking every angle like a miniature stage manager—warmed something deep in his chest.

"You really think this'll help the lodge?" Red asked.

"I dunno," Benny said. "If people come, they'll stay longer and take sleigh rides. If they stay longer, they'll spend money. If they spend money..." He inched the phone to the side and grinned. "It's puppy time! Trust me, Grandpa. This could work."

He did trust the kid, believe it or not. His grand-daughter Nicole was as smart as this little lad, too. Understood advertising and public relations—whatever that was —and things they never needed at Snowberry Lodge before but obviously did now.

As they were finally walking inside, Benny gave him back his phone, looking up at Red with that expression he'd come to know and love for ten years.

He'd never had a son, just two sons-in-law—one died, and the other was a flight risk living in Vermont. And neither of his daughters gave him a grandson, though he adored Gracie and Nicole, his grand-daughters.

But then Gracie made a mistake and, like it some-times happens, from that mistake came the greatest blessing—his namesake, Benedict.

A great-grandson who was well worth the long wait. Red loved him more than he could love any son, and he'd do anything for the kid. Including untangle lights and pretend to be grouchy Santa or whatever Benny called him.

"I like your can-do attitude, Benny-bean," he muttered, a little overcome with affection for the boy.

"And I like your grumpy face," he countered.

"I guess I could be nicer, huh?"

Benny shook his head. "Nope. You're the only Santa I've ever known. You're Santa to me, Grandpa Red. The best Santa in the world."

That hit the old man right in the ribs.

He looked across the property at the big roof of the Snowberry Lodge, lit with the afternoon sun. His father built that roof, and Red had repaired it more times than he could count.

His daughters were raised inside those walls. He'd kissed Cora, his one and only, for the last time outside the mudroom just a few hours before she had a heart attack and met her Maker.

And here he was, pretending to be Santa for a kid who owned Red's whole heart.

"They didn't tell me," Red said softly.

"What?"

"About the lodge being in trouble. MJ, Cindy, Nic, and Gracie."

"The womenfolk, you call them," Benny reminded him. "You always say, 'It's you and me against the womenfolk, Benny-bean.'"

Red chuckled at the dead-on imitation of his old-man voice.

"Maybe they didn't want to worry you," Benny suggested.

"I'm old, not fragile," Red muttered as they walked into the house.

Red peeled off the Santa jacket and flopped into his recliner with a loud sigh. Benny ran upstairs—with the phone, of course.

Just as he was ready to return to his nap, he heard Benny let out a hoot. Oh, yeah. He was "babysitting."

"What is it?" he called without moving.

"We got followers! Five of them in just a few minutes! I must have used the right hashtags!"

Red had no idea what he was talking about, but did someone say hash? He needed a snack after all that work.

He ambled into the kitchen and paused for a moment, for once not forgetting why he'd come in the room. No, he stopped because he was hit with a hammer of love again.

He'd lived in this house his entire eighty-two years on Earth. He knew every worn floorboard, basked in the soft light, and barely noticed the mismatched furniture collected over generations.

He looked around the kitchen, at the original knotty

pine cabinets Pa built by hand. And out the back porch, where he had a view of the lodge grounds, the cabins, and —on clear mornings—all the way to the snowy ridge that cradled Park City.

Benny wanted a puppy...but Red wanted to keep his home.

So, no, he wasn't going to hang up his Santa hat this year. And if Benny wanted him grumpy, he'd be the grumpiest Santa ever.

He stroked his soft old beard and let out a sigh.

Chapter Four

Nicole

The moment Nicole left the airport in Burlington, Vermont, she inhaled crisp, pine-laced air, marveling that something could be both familiar and jarring. It smelled like mountains, felt a little like home, but...everything was different.

Like the Salt Lake Valley, Burlington was surrounded by mountains, but instead of the jagged, majestic drama of the Rockies, Vermont pleased the eye with more moderate slopes.

To the east, the Green Mountains rose gently against the horizon, the distinctive profile of Camel's Hump easy to see as she stepped through the terminal doors. To the west, the beautiful Adirondacks stood layered against the sky, hugged by Lake Champlain.

She totally understood why Dad had moved to Vermont after the divorce, and it wasn't just because his always adventurous parents had come back East to retire in their golden years. It had an earthy mountain atmosphere with beautiful views, with the added touch of quaint New England ambiance.

It was close to his heart, but not the mountain home

where he'd grown up. And, deep down, Nicole hoped that little fact would help her on her own "Operation Sleigh Bells." Only her mission would be a whole lot more challenging than Benny's had been.

"Hey, Nic!"

She turned at the sound of her father's voice, spotting him in the arrival waiting lanes. He waved, opening the driver's door of his white Tacoma.

"Stay there," she called. "I'm coming."

Shouldering her tote and dragging her rolling bag, she navigated the traffic and kept her eyes on her father who, as always, looked great. Jack Kessler was a handsome sixty-year-old, tall and broad, carrying off the puffer jacket and baseball cap with the ease of a man half his age.

His hair had turned mostly silver over the ten years since he'd left Utah, and a lifetime of skiing had made him fit and strong.

"Well, if it isn't my favorite ski bum who doesn't ski," he said, reaching out his arms to hug her.

Good heavens, *that* didn't take long. Nicole rolled her eyes, but he didn't see it as they hugged. "Got that one out of the way," she said. "Can we stop now?"

He chuckled as he gave her a squeeze, and she was reminded that his bear hugs always made her feel about eight years old again. Parting, he smiled, searching her face with eyes the same espresso brown that she saw in the mirror every morning.

She favored him in so many ways—her coloring, her attitude, and, yes, her skiing skills.

So, she should forgive the ski comments. She could have been a great competitive skier, like her father, but one cold and tragic day in January nineteen years ago changed all that. And the guilt for the role he'd played in that accident by pushing her too hard and too fast was never far from the surface for him.

After he tossed her bags in the back, she climbed into the truck. The cab was warm, country music playing low. With some small talk about Thanksgiving and the weather and those first awkward moments of reunion behind them, they pulled away from the airport and headed into the quaint city of Burlington.

The road was flanked by snowy pines and colonial-style homes, all decorated for Christmas with the first of the evening lights starting to twinkle. As they drove and chatted, she let her mind wrap around the request she'd been forming the entire two flights it took to get here.

When would she ask? How? What would he say? It was either completely out of the question or...yeah, he'd help save Snowberry Lodge.

She'd have to wait for the perfect moment.

"You look good, Nic," Jack said, drumming the steering wheel with one hand as he glanced at her. "How's Utah treating you? Heard you guys got a nice little Thanksgiving dump of powder."

"It was not little," she replied. "And there was more on Friday. Base is looking good for Deer Valley."

"Since when do you care about base snow depth at DV?" No surprise, his voice sounded hopeful.

She shot him a look from the passenger seat. "Since I

sell ski gear and there has to be snow in order for people to buy it."

"Fair enough," he conceded.

"How's Grammy?" she asked, easing back to more pleasant subjects. And nothing was more pleasant than Jack's hilarious and wonderful eighty-five-year-old mom.

"Still winning at poker and cheating at bingo." He smiled fondly. "She'd love to see you."

"Sign me up for bingo, please. But how do you cheat?"

"She'll tell you, if she's not busy flirting with all the new arrivals at Pinecrest Village, where she is the unofficial mayor and actually has her own squad."

Nicole gave a soft hoot. "Oh, I love that woman."

"Brace yourself. She's hosting a special Christmas Day brunch with a winter wonderland theme, and has roped me into being the 'guest' speaker."

She laughed. "You can show old Olympics tapes."

"God help us," he said with a self-deprecating laugh. "And how's old Red doing?"

"Cantankerous as ever," she said, always surprised that he asked about anyone at Snowberry before inquiring about Mom.

Nicole rested her head back, feeling the weight of the upcoming conversation pressing on her chest.

"And how's Copper?" Jack asked, thankfully buying her a few more minutes.

Nicole sighed dramatically. "Still a drama king, and the love of my life." At his look, she added, "Literally, so don't ask if I'm dating because the answer is no."

He just smiled as they rode in silence for a bit. "You hungry?" he asked as they got deeper into Burlington, where he lived.

"Starving," she admitted. "Plane peanuts only go so far and my layover in Chicago was frantic."

"Oh, good. I know the perfect place to take you."

As they drove there, she took in the New England Christmas card surroundings—brick buildings with wreaths in every window, a gentle snowfall dancing between gas lamps, and a sweet, slow pace that she really liked.

They pulled into a little café called The Maple Crate, where the windows were fogged up and the smell of coffee practically punched her in the face as soon as the door opened.

Inside, the tables and chairs were mismatched but charming. They settled into a booth with a window view and ordered dinner—Dad chose the maple-glazed meatloaf, but Nicole never could resist a chicken pot pie.

Despite the late hour, they both had coffee, taking a moment to enjoy the warmth of the place.

"So," Jack said after fixing his coffee and taking a sip. "How are things at the lodge?"

Nicole stirred her cream, knowing this was her opening. Where should she start?

"What?" he pressed. "Not good?"

"How can you read me so well?"

He smiled and took a sip. "You're a younger, better-looking version of me. And your expressions are transparent, just like your mother."

Finally, a mention of Mom. She gave him a hard look. "You haven't asked about her, you know."

He swallowed visibly. "How is she?" The question held no harsh tone, no resentment, just genuine curiosity and a little sadness.

"She's okay," she said.

He studied her, his dark gaze piercing hers as a frown pulled. "Are you sure? Is something wrong with her? Is that why you seem...off?"

Oh, yes, the door was wide open and now was the time to step through it. "She's worried—we all are—about how bad business is at the lodge."

"Really?" He inched back, clearly not expecting that answer. "At this time of year? I figured you were booming. And the ski shed, too? I know that's your baby and you do such a great job there, Nic."

"I'm making my numbers, but the lodge has been hit hard. The Grand Hyatt is open and thriving, right smack up against the DV expanded lift lines. It's new and gorgeous, running all kinds of deals, with a spa, and lessons, and blah blah blah."

"But Snowberry has Santa!" He chuckled. "Red's always a big draw."

"It's not enough, Dad. Room nights are just way down. We're not full for Christmas, which has never happened before. We've turned the third-floor suite into storage. Mom is working herself into the ground, and Aunt MJ's pretending like everything's fine. But it's not."

Jack's face shifted slowly—laughter lines relaxing,

gaze narrowing. He didn't speak right away but looked at her with an edge of worry in his eyes.

"There's more," Nicole added.

"She's seeing someone," he said, dropping the statement like a thud.

"What? No." And why did he seem so concerned? Was *that* what worried him?

"I thought that's where you were going," he said, "when you said there was more."

"Well, there is, but not—"

Their food came then, and while they thanked the waiter, her head whirred with the fact that he thought Mom had met someone—and didn't like it. For some reason, that gave her an insane amount of hope. If he cared that much...he might care enough to come back.

"Just tell me, Nic," he insisted as they picked up their silverware.

She took a deep breath of buttery crust and warm chicken. "Mom delayed the tax payment, thinking December would cover it. But..."

"Taxes have gone up?"

She lifted one brow. "Are you kidding? On twenty-five acres zoned for retail and guest accommodations? Mountain views and about ten physical buildings, if you count Starling House, the lodge, stables, and the ski shed, plus—"

"How much?"

She groaned. "A ton. December could cover it if we were packed at full price, but, like Mom says, it's all going to hit us again next year." She felt her shoulders sink. "She's kind of pushing MJ to sell."

He stared at her, and she braced for the natural reaction—shock, dismay, and a long lecture about why that would be the dumbest thing ever.

"Oh, poor Cindy," he whispered under his breath. "That has got to shatter her heart."

The response surprised her—and touched her in an old, old wound. The same wound that was opened when she found her mother looking through pictures of her early years with Jack.

They might have divorced, but they cared deeply for each other.

"Yeah," she said gruffly. "She's pretty wrecked."

With misery etched on every feature, he looked down at his food.

"I'm sorry to hear that," he said. "I know she puts her entire heart and soul into that place." He gave a wry sigh. "Doesn't always make room for anything else."

She had to remember that the issues they'd faced went two ways. Dad loved his job more than anything—but Mom could put running the lodge above everything, too.

For a beat, neither of them spoke, then Nicole leaned in, knowing this was her moment.

"Dad, I think you could help, if you wanted to."

He looked up. "Absolutely. How much does she need?"

She shook her head. "Mom wouldn't take your money."

"Then you take it and give it to her. Don't tell her where it came from."

"I don't keep secrets from her," she said. "Except maybe...well, we could surprise her, and I think I have an idea for how you might help us generate income."

Slowly lowering his fork, he stared at her, the slightest smile tugging. "Why do I think I'm going to hate this?"

She laughed. "Because you might. But hear me out, okay?"

"'Kay."

"Come back, just for the season, and run the sleigh rides again."

He drew back, surprise in his eyes.

"We could advertise the Snowberry Sleigh all over the place and I know it would bring in more business. Families absolutely loved that, and no other resort or lodge has anything like it and, come on, Dad. No one, and I do mean *no one*, on Earth can run that sleigh like you do. You made it such an experience! Flying Jack and the Snowberry Sleigh! It's an event, it's a vibe, it's an—"

"Insane idea," he finished, no smile on his face.

She huffed, out a breath after her speech. "Why?"

"Because..." He shook his head and stared at his meatloaf again. "I can't go back, Nic. And at Christmas? I can't."

"Why not?" she pressed.

"Because Cindy Starling doesn't want to look at me."

She cocked her head. "She never changed her name back, Dad. She's Cindy Kessler, your wife of twenty years. And what makes you think she doesn't want to look at you?"

He shifted in his seat. "Because we ended badly."

"Ten years ago," Nicole said. "And if you showed up to save the lodge and help us fill every empty room for the month of December? She'd forgive you."

"And then give up on me again."

She stared at him, a million emotions swirling through her. It mattered to him more than she realized. She chose her words carefully.

"Um, Dad, I think it was the other way around. You are the one who left. Midlife crisis and a fat ESPN gig. Remember?"

"I left because she gave up on us," he said quietly. "She didn't think she could compete with my job—"

"She couldn't," Nicole said. "No one could."

He swallowed, a storm of emotions in his eyes, even though he was silent.

"So, is that a hard pass?" she guessed, feeling disappointment thud in her chest.

"You're right, Nic, ten years have passed," he said. "And every day during those ten years, I've questioned... what went wrong."

"You wanted to travel," she whispered. "She wanted you home." Was it more complicated than that?

"She gave up too fast, Nic. And, you know, I'm not surprised she's talking about selling the lodge. She's a little bit of a..."

"Quitter?" she filled in when his voice wavered.

"She likes to fix things," he said. "But if it doesn't work right away, she'll quit."

Nicole couldn't argue that about her mother. It was true.

"And me?" he lifted his brows. "I'm a fighter, maybe even to a fault. I refused to give up, even after my accident."

Nicole tried to swallow a bite of chicken, but it stuck in her throat. "Well, that didn't happen to me after my accident."

For a long time, he was quiet, picking at some mashed potatoes. "Yours was different, Nic," he said. "I broke bones. You...almost died."

She exhaled, the memory of the blackness and horror she felt deep in seven feet of darkness and freezing cold, snow in her mouth, her eyes, her lungs...the sound of deathly quiet and her thumping, racing heart.

No, that wasn't an accident. It was a trauma.

"And that's why I don't ski," she said. "Does that make me a quitter, too, Dad?"

His eyes misted as he reached across the table and put his hand on hers. "I'm sorry I made you go down Empire. I'm sorry I pushed you and—"

"You also saved my life," she said, turning her hand to squeeze his fingers. "Because you're not a quitter and you dug through snow and screamed for help and pulled me out alive."

For what felt like an eternity, he stared at her, and she could practically see the dark memory replay in his mind.

"Any chance in heaven or hell you'd ever give me a shot at making it up to you? Hit the slopes and try again?"

She smiled. "No, but I know that won't stop you from asking."

He lifted a shoulder. "It's not too late to try skiing, Nic, or, you know, see someone if you wanted to talk about it."

She shook her head, never wanting to go into therapy after the accident. Her parents had talked about it, but even at nine, she knew she had no desire to re-live what had happened to her on that mountain. Maybe that had been a mistake, but it felt like the right choice to her.

"Do you ever miss skiing?" her father asked.

"Yes, sometimes I do." Why lie? She'd loved skiing... until she didn't.

He angled his head. "It's just that you were so dang good, Nic. Your timing and core strength and speed—"

"Lots of kids have that," she said.

"Not with that reaction time or center of gravity," he countered. "Not with that amazing hand-eye or your focus. And certainly not with that...fearlessness."

She snorted. "Count that one out. The very sight of my old skis can make me tremble with terror."

He closed his eyes with a grunt. "You could get over that, Nic. You could get back on skis. You're only twenty-eight, you could have a lifetime of skiing ahead of you. So many glorious moments, just you and the mountain and—"

She held her hand out. "Are you coming to help us save Snowberry or not?"

Jack leaned back, visibly startled by the abrupt change of subject. "Nicole—"

"You don't have to live at the lodge, though God knows we have the space. Just...show up and do what you do best. Tell your crazy stories, make all the guests laugh and feel enchanted with that Jack Kessler Magic. Make it feel like Christmas again."

He laughed at the description. "That was my first job after I was done skiing, you know."

"I know. That's how you met Mom."

He leaned in, his eyes gleaming. "I took her on the first ride I gave," he said. "And I kissed her right in the middle of Bluebell Crossing that night. Didn't even make it to the old Aspen View trail and I had to have that girl in a liplock."

She was touched that the names for the landmarks were still so easy for him to recall, but how much he still cared for Mom actually made her a little dizzy.

"Well, then maybe you need to get back there and..." *Kiss her again.* "Head up to Bluebell and see how beautiful it is," she said instead.

He sighed again, obviously a little lost in the past, just enough for Nicole to think...she might have a real shot at this.

"What else are you going to do for the next five or six weeks?" she asked.

"Well, for one thing, I'm going to visit my mother with you."

"Tomorrow," she said. "Then we can go home, er, back. And you can ski Deer Valley."

His eyes flashed.

"You'd like that, right, Dad?"

Jack went still. "I'd...love it," he murmured.

For a moment, the café buzzed around them—silverware clinking, chairs scraping, a young couple laughing behind them. Jack stared out the window, lost in thought.

"I'm not sure how it would make me feel to see her again," he said, his voice low.

Nicole blinked against the sudden sting in her eyes. "Neither of you ever moved on."

He smiled without much joy. "Sometimes that's just how it works."

They fell into silence, finishing their food, both deep in thought. Nicole's throat ached, and she could see her plan slipping through her fingers.

After a beat, he said, "I might consider it but..."

She blinked. "But what?"

"I have to be back on Christmas for my mother's brunch."

"But if you ran the rides through Christmas Eve..."

He angled his head with a "don't you get it" look. She didn't.

"It would mean walking out on Christmas...*again*."

Oh. She nodded. "Yeah, I get it. Although if the sleigh rides brought in enough revenue to save December, I'm pretty sure Mom would forgive the repeat of history."

He leaned back, looking at her and thinking. "Then I might consider it."

Her breath caught. "Seriously?"

"On one..."—he held up a finger—"condition."

"What? Anything. Stay somewhere fabulous? Fly First Class? Pick your own horse—Copper's still pretty stubborn, so we might have to rent one. Tell me what it is, Dad, and I'll make it happen."

"You let me teach you how to ski again."

Nicole felt the blood drain from her head, her stomach dropping at the very thought of sliding down a slope. "No."

"Not fly down Centennial," he said. "Just get back on the planks and see how it feels." He sipped coffee like it was no big deal. "We'll go slow. Groomers only. Pizza wedge and all that."

She opened her mouth to say no again, but nothing came out.

"Nic." He reached over and put his hand over hers. "I want to help you overcome that fear. I would never let anything bad happen, I promise. But you're missing out on something wonderful. And if you don't get back on the slopes, it could haunt you for the rest of your life."

"Could? It already has."

"All the more reason to try again. And, honestly, Nic, I would give anything to make it up to you. Let me teach you how..."

"To not be a quitter?" she suggested.

He smiled. "You're not a quitter. I mean, not if you put on a pair of skis and slide down one trail with me. Green. Bunny. You can take Cora's Loop for all I care."

She chuckled at the mention of the tiny hill at Snowberry Lodge that her Grandma Cora used to take her on when she was about two years old.

"I'm not ready, Dad."

"You don't have to be. But I'll come to Snowberry, I'll do the sleigh rides, I'll dress up like Santa, if that's what it takes. If you let me help you reclaim something that used to make you feel so happy and free. There's no joy like skiing, Nic, and you know it."

"None?" she asked on a laugh.

"Well, love," he said with a sad smile. "The old kiss at Bluebell Crossing."

Her heart practically stopped. He *did* still love Mom. And she...yeah, Mom never stopped regretting her divorce.

If Dad came back for a month and they rekindled that romance? Wouldn't Nicole do *anything* for that? Saving Snowberry would just be icing on the cake.

She stared at him for a long time, weighing the pros and cons. The lodge, her parents, a miracle Christmas versus...ice-cold fear.

"Let's go see Grammy tomorrow and go home on Monday," she whispered as the plan formed. "You can stay with me Monday night and we'll surprise everyone Tuesday morning."

A slow smile pulled. "Surprise your mother, you mean. Instead of getting talked out of this insanity."

She laughed. "I think we want the element of surprise on our side, Dad. Is that a yes?" she asked, feeling hope rise. "You'll come to Snowberry for the whole month?"

"You'll put on skis and do one day at DV with me?"

Finally, with her heart pounding and her palms

sweating, she turned her hand and threaded her fingers through his.

She nodded. "Yes."

He threw his head back and pumped a victory fist, making her realize just how much this meant to him. Then he looked at her, faking a frown. "Start with Centennial?"

She smacked his still-raised fist. "Shut up."

Chapter Five

Main Street in Park City sparkled like a snow globe in the afternoon sun, with the brick buildings trimmed in twinkling lights and fresh garlands ribboned around the streetlights. A gentle snow drifted through the crisp mountain air, dusting the sidewalks where bundled-up shoppers ducked in and out of boutiques, art galleries, and toasty cafés.

As Cindy navigated the hill toward Sugarfall, she inhaled the scent of roasted chestnuts mingled with woodsmoke. She threaded her way through clusters of tourists fresh off the slopes, snapping photos beside two-hundred-year-old buildings that captured the charm of a historic mining town.

It was festive but not frantic with a unique alpine magic that she loved even more during the holidays.

Pulling her jacket tighter around her waist, Cindy glanced at the shop windows filled with happy shoppers —so Park City was enjoying a good season.

It was only Snowberry Lodge that felt "light" this year. Light, but not...finished.

After her conversations with MJ and the girls, much introspection, and no small amount of calculations, she was trying to be optimistic about the future. Everyone from Benny to Dad had made it their top priority to "come up with a solution."

In fact, Gracie had implied that's why she wanted Cindy to come to the bakery today—for a conversation she insisted be in person. Turning onto the small side street, she paused in front of her niece's utterly adorable —and also packed—bakery, Sugarfall.

With a smile, she pulled open the heavy glass door and stepped onto the black and white hexagon tile floor, greeted by the aroma of buttery crusts and delectable chocolate.

She never tired of this precious place, a comfy and nostalgic bakery that had become a favorite with tourists and locals alike. Under a white-painted tin ceiling, pastry cases and marble countertops beckoned anyone who had a hint of a sweet tooth.

Behind thick glass, croissants, scones, tarts, and citrus bars were on display with soft lighting that just made them all more irresistible.

Cookies, cupcakes, macaroons, and Gracie's signature creampuffs were front and center, with an entire massive case filled with cakes decorated in holiday colors. In the back, a revolving warming case with seasonal pies turned under soft lights, and the walls were lined with special candies, baking supplies, and trademarked souvenirs.

Along the frosted front windows, bistro tables and cane-backed chairs were nearly filled with guests enjoying coffee and delicious treats.

A single mother at twenty-five, Gracie had used her

natural talent, business acumen, and a few years of formal training as a pastry chef to build a thriving business. She'd taken out a loan and purchased an existing bakery in this location, then rebranded it from top to bottom.

Now nearly as old as Benny, Sugarfall required two professional bakers, some counter staff during peak hours, and one special event manager who worked with hotels and wedding planners all over Park City and beyond.

Not as outgoing as Nicole or as optimistic as her mother, Gracie built her little empire with quiet determination and attention to detail. Few people knew this, because Gracie was soft-spoken, but there was no doubt where Benny got his impressive intelligence. On top of that, she was as sweet as the desserts she offered her guests.

And Cindy loved her niece as much as she loved her own daughter.

Just as Cindy unzipped her jacket, Gracie came out from the back kitchen, holding a small pink box.

"Hi Aunt Cindy!" she called, coming closer and presenting the box. "We made your favorite white chocolate raspberry amaretto cake." She practically sang the dessert's decadent name. "And I saved you a piece because you came to town to see me."

"Thank you, darling." She leaned in and air-kissed her niece, then eyed her suspiciously. "Of course I came. You made it sound intriguing."

"I didn't mean to be cryptic," she said. "I just wanted

you to come with an open mind. Plus, I know you're busy."

Cindy wasn't that busy, to be honest, and the twenty-minute drive was a welcome break from the lodge.

"I was busy wrapping fake presents," Cindy said with a laugh. "Nic's idea to put the sleigh out is great, but Benny in charge of wrapping? Not so great. I helped him put real ribbons on and removed the duct tape. This was a nice escape."

"Good." She guided her toward a small two-top table near a window. "Can I get you a coffee? We brewed that Euro blend you love. With heavy cream and a sugar stick?"

"Of course. Do you have time to join me?"

"Someone does. Sit tight."

What did that mean?

While Cindy took off her jacket, Gracie slipped behind the counter to the coffee station. Cindy glanced around at the happy faces of the Sugarfall clientele, not seeing anyone she knew, but that wasn't unusual.

This was the height of tourist season and the locals who lived and worked here—people Cindy had known her whole life—were all busy serving those tourists.

If they were lucky enough to have that business, she thought glumly.

Her niece came back holding a steaming cup finished with a tall stirring stick laden with sugar crystals that melted into the drink. One thing Gracie never skimped on—sugar.

Placing the cup in front of Cindy, she dropped into the other chair and gave her an expectant look.

Cindy blew on the hot drink but didn't sip. "All right. You've got my full attention. And gratitude for this coffee and cake."

Gracie's smile was tight and weirdly nervous. "Remember how on Thanksgiving we all decided we'd, you know, 'put on our thinking caps' to solve the problems at Snowberry?"

Cindy nodded. "You want to open a second Sugarfall in the lodge? 'Cause I'd say yes."

"Not a bad plan, but no. However, I do talk to a lot of people," she said, brushing the bakery's logo on the front of her flour-dusted apron, once again sounding apprehensive. "And I met someone who might be able to help."

Cindy finally sipped her coffee, lifting a brow. "I'm all ears," she said after swallowing.

"It's a slightly...different approach," she said. "But I think it has potential."

Cindy studied her lovely niece, waiting for more.

"There's a man who comes in here once in a while," she said, lowering her voice to a whisper. "He owns several properties throughout the West and has invested in a few boutique hotels around Utah. We were talking and I mentioned Snowberry and told him a little about our history and...our issues."

"You told a stranger?"

"An *advisor*," she corrected. "He wasn't surprised, honestly, and really knows the market and property values. Everything. I think he might help with an investment."

Cindy shot a brow up. "An investor? Would it be like a loan? I don't want to saddle us—or you, in the future—with debt and interest." And she didn't need *another* bill to pay.

"I know and I appreciate that," Gracie said. "I only just finished paying off my bank loan and it was a bear. But this man has real estate and hospitality experience, not like a bank lender. He'd be more of a partner."

"A partner?"

"Well, think of him like one of those Shark Tank guys, only for property instead of products. He said he would—"

"I can't wait any longer."

Startled, Cindy sucked in a soft breath and looked up —way up—into the face of a man smiling down at her.

"You must be Aunt Cindy. I'm Henry." He held out a hand to her. "It's a pleasure to meet you."

As if her body had a will of its own, Cindy stood slowly, taking hold of the strong, slightly calloused hand that gripped hers. Even standing to her full five-foot-six, she still had to look up a bit to meet a blue-gray gaze of a man about her age, with a head of salt-and-pepper hair and an even more peppery close-cropped beard.

He wore rimless glasses and a navy cable-knit sweater which all gave him kind of a professorial look. A slate-colored wool coat, about a shade darker than his eyes, hung over his arm.

"Hello...Henry," she managed, taken aback by the sheer power of the man. "Yes, I'm Cindy Kessler."

"Henry Lassiter." He shook her hand, never taking his inviting gaze from hers. "Gracie's told me so much about you—and your lovely property. Full disclosure, I sneaked over there yesterday, bought a pair of gloves from the shop, and took the nice young woman's advice to stroll the property. It's one in a million. Can we talk?"

For a moment, she just stared at him, feeling a strange weakness in her knees. And a sense of...familiarity. She didn't know the man and certainly would have remembered meeting him had she bumped into him at Snowberry Lodge yesterday.

"May I?" he added when she didn't answer, gesturing to the table.

"Sit right here, Henry," Gracie said, instantly vacating her seat. "I'll bring you a coffee and let you two get acquainted."

Gracie whisked away and Henry folded his coat over the back of the chair. While he did, Cindy looked past him at her reflection in the pastry case, suddenly smoothing a hand through her blond waves, wishing she'd taken a little more care with her makeup. She had no idea she'd meet a handsome stranger today.

Her cheeks flushed at the thought—the man wanted to invest in her property, not ask her on a date. But still, he had a strong presence, and something was *so* familiar about him. She couldn't pinpoint it.

"Have you been in Park City for very long?" she asked as he settled in, certain she must have met him somewhere. Maybe at a business owners networking event or even something social in town.

"I have a home in the canyons—Little Cottonwood, on the outskirts of Salt Lake. I assume you're familiar with it?"

She nodded, knowing the very upscale suburb. "You have *a* home?" she laughed softly. "How many do you have?"

He chuckled. "Just two that I live in. The other is in southern California, where I go when I desperately need a beach."

Gracie came right back with his coffee, her eyes bright. "I really hope you two hit it off," she said. "Henry might have some good ideas, Aunt Cindy. I hope it...well, I hope you agree."

When she left, they looked at each other, both laughing at the awkward moment.

"I take it you're not thinking about an investor?" he guessed.

"Not really."

He smiled, lifting his mug in a mock toast. "Here's to new solutions to old problems."

He held her gaze with a glimmer in his eyes and, she couldn't help noticing, no ring on his left hand.

Cindy just answered with her own smile, sipping her coffee and letting him lead the conversation.

"So," he said, bracing his elbows on the tabletop. "You need money."

She laughed. "That's an auspicious opening."

"Not for me," he replied. "I'm an investor. And I invest in properties exactly like yours."

Easing back, she took a slow breath, sensing she'd need her wits about her for this conversation. "How much has Gracie told you?" she asked.

"Enough for me to know that Snowberry Lodge has been in your family for generations," he said. "And you'd very much like to keep it that way. I can help you."

She nodded, purposely not adding to that.

"Like I said, I visited yesterday."

"You should have introduced yourself," she said, keeping her voice warm so it didn't sound accusatory. "I would have loved to have shown you around."

"I'll come back," he said easily. "But I wanted to meet you on neutral ground first, and find out what you need, exactly."

Where did she start? "I need more guests than I have now," she said, opting for honesty over any witty comebacks. "We're running at a...lower than normal capacity, and that's odd for December."

"Do you know why?"

"Two words: Grand Hyatt."

He nodded but looked skeptical.

"Do *you* know why?" she countered.

"I invest in high-velocity hospitality zones—locations where space is finite, demand is infinite, and timing is everything."

She lifted her brows at the smooth description. "My sister and I own a hundred-year-old lodge with more original plumbing than I care to admit. I don't think it's the same business model."

"I do," he countered. "Park City is high-velocity and Snowberry Lodge is situated on a spot that, well, God's just not making any more land like that. And you have something very few properties on this mountain or in these canyons have or can ever offer."

"Unobstructed views?" she guessed, suspecting he didn't really know how many places had great views.

"Authentic, heartbreaking, impossible-to-find *charm*."

She let out a sigh. "You sound like my sister," she said. "She believes that's enough to fill the beds. I'm not sure I agree. Tourism is changing and people want contemporary ambiance and modern conveniences. They want ease and flash and hot tubs with cocktail service. That's not what Snowberry offers."

Henry nodded thoughtfully, considering her words. "I look for places with soul, Cindy," he said. "And I invest in them, and step back, allowing the owners to do whatever it was they've always done to maintain that soul."

"I like the sound of that," she admitted. "And you saw...soul at Snowberry?"

He chuckled. "Oodles of it. From the rooflines to the stone stairs. The cabins are precious, the stables are quaint, and the lodge itself looks like a Hallmark movie."

"Well, don't look too closely. The roof leaks, the stone stairs are cracked, the cabins need insulation, and no one is filming any movies at Snowberry." She sipped her coffee. "But I like that you see what we love about it."

He leaned in. "All that needs to be fixed is money,"

he said. "And that's what I can give you. I keep a small portfolio and work closely with the owners. I don't believe in modernizing a classic—I believe in enhancing it."

"And you want to invest in Snowberry?" she asked, hating that hope rose in her.

He smiled. "If you're open to it. I'd be willing to put in two-hundred-fifty thousand for renovations and upgrades in exchange for a small percentage of revenue. Not ownership. Not even partnership. Just a percentage."

Two hundred and...*what?* Cindy blinked, not hearing much of anything after that.

She let the number settle on her, suddenly imagining everything fixed, upgraded, and improved. There would be money to spare to pay the yearly tax bills. That wouldn't get them on the lift line, but if they had a beautiful warm bus instead of an old van...

"How small a percentage?" she asked, her voice thick.

"We'll work out the details." He flicked his hand. "Nothing that would impact your life."

But everything he said would impact her life. In a very good way. Two hundred and fifty thousand? "It would...change my life."

"I don't *want* to change your life, Cindy," he said with a warm smile. "I want to make it better. You talk to your sister—I understand Gracie's mother is your partner? No, um, husband to join in the decision-making?"

He sounded a little hopeful, and she wasn't sure how to take that. Hopeful he didn't have to contend with another opinion or...something else?

"I'm divorced," she said.

"Same," he replied. "Eight years. How many for you?"

"Ten." She searched his face, wondering about the woman he'd married...and divorced.

"It's hard," he said softly. "People talk about divorce so casually, but it's like a death. Grief lasts a long time. At least it did for me," he added quickly. "I don't know if it was the same for you."

The same? She was *still* grieving the loss of Jack Kessler. "It wasn't easy," she admitted.

"You ever consider remarrying?" he asked.

"Too busy," she replied. "Also, too old."

He laughed and shook his head. "You are not. But I get the busy. Sometimes I think I just worked really hard to fill the dead space."

"Do you have kids?" She didn't know why she was asking personal questions, but she was curious.

"I have two sons," he said. "One is close and does a lot of business with me. The other is...estranged."

"I'm sorry," she said. "That has to be difficult."

He gave a tight smile. "I keep hoping, but...we'll see." He shifted in his seat. "Tell me more about the lodge."

"I suppose you want to know fixed operating expenses, overhead, variable per room costs. That kind of thing."

"Someday I will," he said. "But now, I'd like to know the history, and how it got so charming. Tell me about your grandparents, and your father. The reason people come and why they stay. The legends, the ghost stories, the famous guests, and what makes the place... sticky."

"Sticky?" She drew back, not expecting to be asked about any of that. "My sister's overuse of bacon fat makes it sticky."

He laughed. "I mean what keeps people coming back. Obviously, the food's good."

"The food's amazing," she said. "The staff is small— just Nina and Pedro, a wonderful couple who have worked for us for seven or eight years. They keep the place clean and running in tip-top shape. I think they'll want to retire soon, so there's that issue. What else did you ask? Legends? Well, during the 2002 Olympics, Bode Miller stayed at Snowberry Lodge, but he and my ex-husband were friends."

He lifted a brow. "Really?"

"Jack, my ex, was an Olympic-level skier. Bode was probably our most famous guest. Ghosts? None that I know of, but lots of folks who stay in Cabin Four say they hear singing in the middle of the night." She gave a conspiratorial smile. "I don't have the heart to tell them it's the water heater."

He chuckled, and with each passing moment, she grew more relaxed. Could this guy be for real? Could he truly have that kind of cash to give Snowberry?

Well, not give. *Invest.* She couldn't forget that this money wasn't free.

He asked more questions, told her a little bit about himself and where some of his other investments were in

Utah and other places in the West, talking until their coffee grew cold.

Finally, they both leaned back for a mutual and comfortable goodbye.

"I'd love to visit the lodge again," he said as they stood. "Can I call you?" He handed her his cell phone. "Just type in your number."

She looked down, forced her aging eyes to focus, and saw "Cindy at Snowberry" on a white screen. It seemed harmless and sweet, plus Gracie knew him. She could show him the lodge again, couldn't she? That wasn't...committing.

She typed in her number and handed the phone back to him, their hands brushing.

The reaction that Cindy felt was all too real and, once again, familiar.

"You remind me of someone," she confessed, now comfortable enough to say that to him. "Are you sure we've never met?"

"I would remember," he said with just a sweet enough smile to make her feel...seen. "I'll call you, Cindy."

When was the last time a man said those words to her? Well, probably after her last fight with the county inspector over that roofing permit. The roof that would have to be replaced...with money she didn't have.

But Henry Lassiter did.

They said goodbye, but she lingered, hoping to talk to Gracie. Looking in the back, she saw her niece was meeting with a couple about a wedding cake.

When she caught her eye, she gave Gracie a wave and a thumb's up, then headed out with a bounce in her step. Maybe things were turning around. Maybe they wouldn't have to sell, just...get an investor. And a good-looking one at that.

On the drive home, she got a call from her bedding supplier—prices were going up in January—and another from a travel agent who was supposed to bring in a ski tour but had to pull out.

Dang it all, she thought as she turned into the long drive at Snowberry Lodge. She'd never needed that two hundred and fifty more than right now.

Stepping inside the back kitchen door, she got a whiff of that very bacon her sister loved as she kicked off her boots in the mudroom.

"Hello?" she called.

Benny came running into the kitchen, sock-sliding at the mudroom door. "Did you know I have an Uncle Jack?"

She looked up from her boot, a little surprised that would be news to Benny, who picked up every nuance of every conversation. "Yes. Why?"

"He's here!"

Cindy froze. "What?"

She looked right over Benny's shoulder, and there stood the man she'd once promised to love, honor, and cherish till death parted them. She blinked, her head suddenly light, her heart dropping to the floor, and her brain registering one insane thought.

Jack. *That's* who Henry Lassiter reminded her of.

Confident, handsome, look-right-into-your-soul Flying Jack Kessler.

"What are you doing here?" she croaked.

"Nicole convinced me to come back for a month and run the sleigh rides."

She stared at him, nothing making sense or registering. *Nicole...did...what?*

He took a step closer. "I know you're in a bind, Cin. And I'm here to help."

For a moment, she couldn't hear or think or breathe. All she could do was look up at a man she'd once loved so much it physically hurt.

"I can run the sleigh rides and we'll pack this place with happy guests and paying passengers, enough to save your December and cover that tax bill." After a beat of silence, he dipped a little lower and she could have sworn he was going to kiss her. "Is that okay?"

What could she say? No? And why did every cell in her body just melt like a snowflake on sun-warmed stone? "That's...that's..."

"A great idea, right, Mom?" Nicole swept in, her dark eyes glinting with hope and...mostly just hope. Hope that she would agree to this wild and wrong and...*wonderful* idea.

Cindy nodded and managed a deep breath. "It really is," she whispered.

And, oddly enough, she meant it.

Chapter Six

Red

Red knew better than to go for thirds. He knew it right around the time he went for seconds, honestly. But MJ's rosemary beef stew had been bubbling on the stove all afternoon, and by the time he'd torn into his second hunk of crusty sourdough, slathered with whipped garlic butter, he'd already lost the will to resist.

Now he was stuffed like a Christmas goose and trying not to groan in front of his daughters, granddaughters, great-grandson, and the man he used to call son-in-law... back when he liked him.

"Well, that might be the best thing I've eaten since your mother's beef bourguignon," he declared, leaning back in the head chair at the long pine kitchen table.

MJ beamed across the table, her cheeks flushed from the compliment—or maybe just the heat from the oven. "That's high praise, Dad."

Red didn't respond. He just reached for his water glass and caught Jack glancing at Cindy. Looking at her like...like he shouldn't have left.

Well, I coulda told you that ten years ago, ya big lug nut.

Cindy was quieter than usual, probably still in shock

that Nicole had gone to Vermont, come home five days early and brought...baggage.

Red tried to keep his face neutral as he secretly studied his former son-in-law.

Jack had aged, sure—salt in his hair, some creases around his once-boyish grin. But there was still that glimmer of charm and that casual confidence that came with a childhood of winning and a decade or so in front of the cameras.

Jack had always been the kind of man who could talk a bear out of its salmon. And, once upon a time, Red had admired that about him. Now Red just couldn't forgive the other man for what he'd put Cindy—and Nicole—through.

With a satisfied sigh, Jack folded his napkin next to his plate. "Still can't beat a good family dinner," he said with the easy tone of someone trying too hard not to make waves. "Thank you, MJ."

"You can't be done yet, Uncle Jack," Gracie said. "I brought home a mountain of macaroons."

Benny snickered. "Macaroon mountain. Sounds like a new trail at Deer Valley."

"And speaking of DV trails," Jack said, leaning in and looking at Nicole. "Do they know?"

"Know what?" Cindy asked.

Nicole gave a tight smile. "I, um, agreed to hit the slopes with Dad tomorrow morning."

For a moment, no one said a word. There was nothing but shocked silence until Nicole gave a dry laugh. "So apparently pigs *can* fly."

"No, but Jack Kessler can," MJ said, beaming at him. "Good for you, Nic. I, for one, think it's a great idea."

But Cindy looked stunned. "Are you sure, honey?"

"No," she admitted on a chuckle. "But...the man drives a hard bargain, and I couldn't say no."

Really? Red sat up a little. She'd been saying "no" to skiing ever since that day she went down a tree well and darn near never came up again. Just thinking about how they'd almost lost little Nicole in one of the deep, hidden holes that form in the snow under conifers made him shudder.

"I'm surprised, that's all," Cindy said, reaching down to pull her phone from her pocket. "Oh, excuse me," she said, glancing at the screen. "This is the reservation line."

She got up to slip into her office around the corner and MJ immediately stood to start cleaning up.

"Let us help, Mom," Gracie said.

"Absolutely," Jack agreed, getting up. "I have to move before climbing Mount Macaroon."

When the four of them left the table, Benny plowed a bony elbow into Red's arm. "Gimme your phone," he demanded in a whisper. "Quick, quick."

Red reached behind him on the windowsill where he'd left it, handing it to the boy with a warning eye, whispering, "You should tell your mother what you're doing."

"What *we're* doing, Grandpa. And I can't because she will have a cow. Look! We have five thousand followers!" He tapped the screen and grinned up. "Five thousand and thirty. Do you know what that means?"

"I have no idea what any of this means," he admitted.

Cindy burst back into the room, holding her own phone like it was a golden ticket. "Guess what? We just booked two of the cabins for Christmas week!"

Everyone stopped talking.

"Really?" Gracie asked, turning off the running water.

"Two full week stays," Cindy said, practically dancing. "Someone named Bryant from Ogden and another family from Washington State. Said they saw Snowberry Lodge on social media and just *had* to spend Christmas here."

Red raised his eyebrows. "On social media?"

"I bet it's the sleigh!" Nicole exclaimed. "Bri told me that since we dragged it out there, all the ski shed customers are taking pictures on it."

Red glanced down at Benny, who was practically vibrating, and gave the kid a secret wink.

Benny nearly fell off his chair as he fluttered his little feet with uncontained excitement.

"Are you all right, honey?" Gracie asked, coming around the large island. "Do you have to..." She didn't finish but lifted her brows.

"He's potty trained, for heaven's sake," Red said. "He's just excited."

"About what?"

"These reservations," Red told her. "Right, Benny-bean?"

Benny just nodded, no doubt because he knew—they

both knew—exactly where those two reservations had come from. *Hashtag Ho Ho Ho.*

"I'm excited, too, Benny!" Cindy exclaimed. "I mean, I know it's just two, but I don't know. I feel...optimistic."

As they all chattered about it, Benny leaned closer. "Come on, Grandpa. Let's sneak out and do one more. We gotta strike while we're trending."

"We're what?"

"I mean, not really trending," Benny continued in a whisper. "But I have an idea for the sleigh again. You can talk and I'll edit it all together in CapCut."

Red rubbed his temple. "Cap-what?"

"Please, while my mom is busy."

Red nodded and stood, taking his plate to the sink. "Benny and I are going to make sure all the lights are working on the sleigh," he said. "Since it seems to be doin' its job."

They stepped into the chilly night, the snow falling gently over the trees like powdered sugar on cupcakes. The sleigh sat under a canvas tarp, but Benny pulled it off, then did something on Red's phone and suddenly the fairy lights glowed on the rails.

How did he...

Benny snagged the Santa hat from the back and flipped it to Red. "Wardrobe, please."

Muttering under his breath, Red tugged it over his bald head.

"You ready?" Benny asked.

"Born ready."

"Okay, this one's called *Grumpy Santa Won't Come*

Inside. You just sit in the sleigh and grumble about not coming in until there's peace on Earth."

Red blinked. "That's kind of political."

"It's festive," Benny corrected.

Before Red could respond, the side door creaked open and Jack stepped out, pulling on his coat.

"Evening," Jack said, approaching cautiously. "Since I'm so involved in the sleigh, I thought I'd join you two."

Red looked at Benny, who shrugged and nodded.

"Only if you can keep a secret," Red said. "Benny's breakin' house rules for the good of mankind."

"And for a puppy that Aunt Cindy promised to get me!"

Jack frowned, coming closer. "Come again?"

"TikTok," Benny said, scrambling down from the sleigh and holding out his phone. "Do you know what that is, Uncle Jack?"

He chuckled. "Yes. I'm old, not dead."

"'Cause Grandpa didn't."

"Well, I'm closer to dead," Red said wryly. "Just tell him, Benny."

Benny held out the phone and spewed a long story about followers and hashtags and trending. *And* a promised puppy.

Jack didn't really respond until he clicked through a few of Benny's little masterpieces, smiling, then chuckling, and finally laughing out loud.

"The Santa who's had enough of Christmas." He shook his head and grinned at Benny, then Red. "This is brilliant. Why are you keeping it a secret?"

"I'm not supposed to know how to use any of it," Benny said. "I don't have a phone. And my mom will kill me, not give me any presents, and I want that puppy."

Jack's shoulders moved in a soft laugh. "If technology doesn't work out, Ben, you can be a lawyer. Also, not giving you a phone is like not giving Einstein a slide rule."

"But it's a rule and I'm breaking it. Please don't tell anyone. Please."

"I'll keep your secret."

"Thanks," Red said. "'Cause it appears to be working."

"Oh, *you're* the social media that got the reservations," he said, his eyes flickering. "That's awesome. Way to go, Grumpy. And...Steven Spielberg, Jr."

"Who's that?" Benny asked.

"Doesn't matter, but I'd love to help," Jack said. "Why don't we do one tomorrow with me in that old carriage driving costume? I assume you still have that getup that makes me look like I stepped out of a Charles Dickens novel?"

"I think so," Benny said. "Would it be in a box with a big, tall black hat?"

Jack made a face. "I look ridiculous in that thing but, yes, that's my carriage gear."

"Cool," Benny said. "Now I'm going to go over there and start recording. Grandpa, you know what to do. Jack, cover for us if my mom comes out."

He and Red shared a look, then both nodded. When Benny scrambled away, Jack turned to Red. "Good thing you're doing with this kid, Red."

Red put his hand on the side of the sleigh. "Good thing *you're* giving up your Christmas to help us."

Jack nodded, silently, then added, "I admit, I get the feeling you aren't overjoyed to see me."

"'Cause I'm not." He struggled to climb up, and Jack gave him a gentle hand and helped him onto the front bench, Red landing on the leather with a grunt. "But now you're here."

"I have to be back in Vermont for Christmas Day," he said, looking up at Red.

"Huh." Red said. "Just like old times."

Jack grimaced. "Look, I want to help the lodge. I want to—"

"Okay, Grandpa—ready? Look annoyed."

He glanced at Jack. "That's not hard."

"That's not the line, Grandpa!"

Jack stepped back and Red muttered, "You people owe me hazard pay."

"Rolling!"

Red looked angrily into the night air. "I'm not comin' in until someone brings me a cookie the size of my face."

Jack cracked up but Red stayed in character, holding his scowliest face—and God had given him plenty of those.

Benny, the evil genius, had Red do the whole thing three more times after Jack whispered that he'd be right back. A minute later, he returned with a couple of Gracie's cookies, one of which Benny filmed so close he had to have gotten sugar on the phone.

He made Red put one on his nose, hold one next to

his face, and juggle them. He dropped two just as the door opened and Gracie called for Benny to come in so they could head home up the hill.

"Where you staying?" Red asked Jack.

"For now, MJ put me in Cabin One, but with what you two are doing? I'll probably end up crashing on Nicole's sofa because Snowberry'll be booked."

"From your lips," he said, slowly climbing down from the sleigh.

Benny had gone inside and the two of them stood in the snowy silence for a moment.

Jack cleared his throat. "Look, Red. I know I don't deserve much. Probably don't deserve this second chance at being nearby. But I have a lot of making up to do and I'm hoping to help."

Red didn't say a word. How could he? He had ten years of anger built up against this man.

"You, uh, still hate me, huh?" Jack asked.

Red laughed at the candor. "Li'l bit. But that doesn't make you special. I hate everybody." He added a wink. "Why do you think they call me Grumpy Santa?"

With that, he headed back inside, not yet ready to forgive, forget, or let Jack Kessler off the hook.

Chapter Seven

Nicole

Nicole tugged her ski jacket tighter around her chest as the shuttle van rolled to a gentle stop near the base of Deer Valley.

Bri grinned widely, eyeing her in the rearview mirror from the driver's seat. "How ya feeling, girl?"

Nicole swallowed and glanced over at her dad, who was also grinning like a kid on Christmas morning. She rolled her eyes.

"You two are both entirely too excited about this. I'm going down the bunny hill and trying not to die. It's not some big comeback story."

Jack shrugged and glanced out the window to hide his smile. "I didn't say a word. I'm just happy to be getting out on the slopes with you, kid."

"And I'm beyond jealous," Bri said on a groan as she pulled the shuttle van up to the resort entrance to drop them off. "That powder is calling my name."

"It'll be there when your shift ends," Nicole said with a smile as she grabbed her helmet off the seat next to her.

"But it'll be all skied over and I want first tracks." She stuck her tongue out playfully.

Jack chuckled. "And we're going to make them."

First tracks? Ugh. Nicole just hopped out of the van with a wave of her gloved hand. "Bye, Bri. Sell lots while I'm gone today."

"Ski like the wind! Have fun, Flying Jack!" Brianna blew her a kiss and Nicole stepped away, trying to ignore the fact that her knees felt wobbly at the very sight of the lift base.

Beyond them, the mountain rose in layered folds of white, dusted with fresh powder that glittered in the morning sun. The air was filled with the distant whoosh of skis carving downhill and the cheerful clatter of poles.

Guests in brightly colored jackets bustled between the base lodge and the lifts, laughter and music from outdoor speakers floating through the cold like confetti.

Nicole's stomach twisted as she marched next to Dad, the scent of hot cocoa wafting from a nearby stand clashing with the old, familiar knot of nerves curling beneath her layers.

She hoisted the pair of skis she grabbed from the shed over her shoulder and tried to take a calming breath. Maybe the coffee she'd downed before leaving was a bad idea after all, because all she felt were jitters and a hint of heartburn.

"You okay?" Jack asked, walking beside her with the skis he'd chosen for the day effortlessly resting on his shoulder.

"I can't believe I'm doing this, Dad."

Jack notched his chin toward the medley of groomed green ski runs that wound down from the first-level lifts.

"No worries, Nic. You were ripping those when you were three."

"I was fearless at three."

He stopped, bracing her shoulder with a strong hand, the kind of steadying support she always loved from her father. It hit her right then how much she missed it—missed him—and how deeply she wanted to show this man what she was made of.

"Hey, the second you say you're done, we leave."

"I'm done," she joked. "Can we go get pancakes instead?"

"Just try," he urged. "Come on. Let's get you locked into your skis and see how it feels to just...glide around. Sound good?"

Actually, it sounded horrible, but she followed him to the snow-covered hill where people were lacing up their bindings and shuffling to the lift lines.

The morning sun peeked through the frosted pines, casting a soft glow over the pristine white slopes of Deer Valley. Snow clung to every tree branch like thick icing, and the air sparkled with the crisp magic of early winter.

"I forgot how much gear was involved with this sport," Nicole muttered, fumbling with her two—yes, two—layers of gloves and shoving her neck warmer over her braided hair. "You have to bring a suitcase-worth of clothes just to get out here."

Jack stood a few paces away, adjusting his gloves and laughing softly. He looked every inch the former Olympian, even at sixty—still tall, still confident, still radiating that unshakable peace she remembered from her childhood. He'd always seemed unbreakable on skis, despite the injury that derailed his competitive dreams.

He hadn't let that stop him from skiing again.

She, on the other hand, felt like she was about to unravel nineteen years after...that day.

She scanned the mountain, which was peppered with skiers and teeming with the excitement of a big early season snow.

Her gaze fell on a section of trees, and her heart rate kicked up. She remembered the feeling of going face first into a tree well—not there, but much, much higher. She easily recalled feeling trapped, stuck, *terrified*. She hadn't broken anything, but the fear had calcified in her bones.

Jack looked over and smiled. "You good?"

"Yeah. Fine. I'm guessing you want to start by going up Carpenter?" She nodded toward the set of main lifts—Carpenter and Silver Lake.

"You think you're ready for Success?" he asked, referring to the quintessential green run that took beginner skiers down from the top of Carpenter lift to the base.

"It's a long green," she said, the knowledge more from conversations she'd had with Brianna and customers than her dimmed memory.

"You're right," he said quickly. "Why don't we start with Snowflake?"

She chuckled softly. "I've never seen anyone over the age of five take that lift."

"It's perfect." He skied over and crouched beside her. "We're taking it slow this time. Just the bunny slope.

We're not even doing turns yet—just relearning how to shift your weight and get used to the skis. You'll be fine."

Nicole nodded stiffly.

He gestured up the hill where the tiny, two-seater lift took beginners to the top of a mostly flat, wide slope. "Come on, Nic. It'll be fun."

Of course, Snowflake had no lift line, so they got right on.

She let him guide her onto the lift. It wasn't steep. It wasn't fast. The other lift riders were all younger than Benny. *Much* younger than Benny, who could ski, but didn't really have a passion for it.

It wasn't anything like that black diamond run from two decades ago. And yet her palms were sweaty in her gloves.

At the top of the hill, the world opened up in soft curves of snow.

Nicole stepped off the lift and skidded slightly, her boots clunky in the bindings, her legs leaden and stiff on the skis.

The slope below wasn't steep, but from up here, it looked vast—an untouched sheet of white stretching down toward the base, dotted by a scattering of toddlers in neon snowsuits and parents crouching behind them.

The cold nipped at her cheeks, but sweat was already prickling under her layers. Around her, ski instructors called encouragement, poles clicked, and laughter rang out, carefree and echoing—so opposite the weight dragging in her chest.

Before they started, Jack stood at the top of the rise, squinting at the bottom.

"Five bucks?" he said, fighting a smile.

She smiled, too, remembering their old bet—his first form of bribery to get her to take a run that scared her. They always bet five bucks on who'd get to the bottom first.

"I'll take that bet," she said, more to honor the special memory than any notion that she'd beat him on this pathetic little hill.

They started down. It was seriously flat, but Nicole was terrified. She wobbled, caught her balance, wobbled again.

Jack skied alongside her slowly, offering gentle corrections. "Weight on your downhill foot. That's it."

Her downhill foot. The one that felt like it weighed fifty pounds? She nodded, trying to concentrate, but feeling so, so unsteady.

"Eyes ahead, Nic," he said. "Where you look is where you'll go."

So...*don't look at a tree.* "'Kay," she managed to say.

"There you go, honey," he cooed. "Trust your body. It knows what to do."

It did, once upon a time. Today? She slid a little and whimpered.

"Pick your line and trust it, Nic." he continued. "You want this. You know you want this. Steady, steady..."

Her ski veered left, she overcorrected, and panic seized. Leaning forward, her skis caught a little too much speed, and her old fear bloomed like frostbite in her chest.

"Dad!" she gasped.

He tried to ski over, but before he reached her, Nicole tumbled sideways into a fluffy pile of snow just off the run.

She lay still for a moment, humiliated, snowflakes melting on her cheeks.

Jack coasted over, worry on his face. "You okay?"

Nicole sat up, brushing snow off her jacket. "I'm fine. Just..." She couldn't admit she was scared of this. There were scarier slopes on the Snowberry Lodge property, not that she'd ever attempted back-country skiing.

Jack crouched beside her. "You did great, Nic. Honestly. That was a solid first run."

"I fell."

"Everybody falls."

But not everybody almost dies, she thought.

Jack sat down on the snowbank next to her. He raised his goggles onto his helmet and studied her with concern and care. "Come on, honey. That wasn't bad. You fell onto your side, just like I taught you when you were young."

She tugged at her face covering, getting an icy breeze on her skin.

"I remember," she said softly, grabbing clumps of snow with her gloved hands. "You used to always say, 'If you're not falling, you're not trying.'" She said in a playful, mocking voice. "I wanted to strangle you."

He laughed heartily, patting her back. "It's true, though. And you always got back up."

"Until...I didn't." She looked down at the rental skis, sprinkling them with the fistfuls of snow in her hands. "Nic..."

She let out a slow breath, staring at the slope. "I feel like I let you down. Back then. When I quit skiing."

Jack blinked. "Nicole. We've talked about this a million times. You didn't let me down. You had an accident."

She closed her eyes. "*You* had an accident, Dad," she reminded him. "I had a trauma."

"You think hearing a bone crack and knowing what shattered was a chance to stand on the podium at the Olympics wasn't traumatic?"

Nodding, she didn't fight that, but eventually looked up at him.

"I never forgot it," she said on a rasp. "I never forgot how black it was in the snow. How I couldn't breathe. How I knew—at nine years old—that I was dying. It etched fear on me and this...this..." She grabbed a gloveful of snow and flicked it in the air. "This brings it all back. And these." She tried to move the ski stuck in the snow. "The very air on this mountain makes it all come back to me."

His whole face registered the pain. "I should have pushed harder for you to have some therapy."

"No, no, Dad. I didn't want it and as a kid, I didn't realize it would linger. I just wanted to...not ski anymore. Then I was—I *am*—fine."

"I'm so sorry, Nic. I'm sorry you went through that."

She sighed, watching the bunny slope in front of her, observing a cute interaction between parents and their toddler son, wobbling his way down the hill.

"It wasn't your fault," she said.

"Taking you up the Empire lift was," he replied. "Letting you ski ahead of me was. Acting like you were my protégé training for the Olympics? All on me."

She swallowed, emotion tugging at her heart.

He scratched the back of his neck, adjusting his helmet. "I should never have let you go through those trees. It was too steep."

She sat very still, the mountain and skiers around them disappearing as she let herself slide back to that day. The moment her body went flying forward into all that loose, deep snow around the tree, sinking and sinking face first into ice-cold blackness, trapped and disoriented and deeper with every panicked move.

All she could taste was snow and all she could hear was the hammer of her heart, then a muffled voice. Desperately trying to move the skis that she hoped were still visible, her legs paralyzed by the snowpack that trapped her.

She opened her mouth to call for Dad, but that just filled it with suffocating, drowning snow.

"Don't go there," he said softly, reaching for her hand. "Don't relive it, Nic."

"Don't you?"

He choked a bitter laugh. "Yeah. Of course I do."

She searched his face, hating that her trauma

haunted him, too. "But you saved me, Dad. You dug through that snow, you calmed me down, you cleared my lungs, you..." She realized she was crying as her voice cracked. "You saved me."

"And now I dragged you up here to relive it all," he said, his voice rich with self-derision.

"You're trying to help," she assured him. "You want me to love what you love. And the irony is that I *do* love it, but..." She bit her lip, hating that she had to tell him the truth. "Dad, I can't do this. It's just not worth putting myself through the stress. I know we made a deal but—"

A voice called from behind them. "Everybody okay over here?"

Nicole turned and saw a ski patrol officer sliding to a graceful stop. He pushed up his goggles and smiled, giving her a good look at a handsome face and eyes that matched the sky behind him.

She took in the sight of a man in his late twenties or so, dark blond tousled hair under his helmet, rugged stubble, and the official red jacket that looked out of place on the bunny hill.

Jack managed to get up, using his pole for leverage. "We're all good here, just taking a break."

Nicole did the same, forcing herself to get her skis straight, and not look like the bunny slope loser she was.

"Nothing's hurt but my pride." She pushed her goggles off and tried to smile. "It heals easily."

His blue eyes glinted. "First day?"

She lifted a shoulder. "Essentially."

"Ah," he said, nodding, then looked at her dad. "Baptism by snow. I'm Cameron, by the way."

Her father extended a gloved hand. "Jack. This is Nicole, my daughter. And thanks for checking on us, son."

The other man leaned back on his skis, staring at her father. "Wait a second. I know that voice. Are you...Jack Kessler?"

"Guilty."

"You're like a local ski legend," he said. "Very cool surprise. Good to have you here, Mr. Kessler."

Nicole watched her father wave a hand and brush off the recognition. "Good to be back at DV. I got my ski legs here."

Cameron beamed. "I used to study your racing tapes when I was attempting a Super-G. Still one of the best I've ever seen."

Jack gave a modest shrug, wrapping his arm around Nicole's shoulders. "That was a long time ago. Now I'm just an old has-been having an easy day with my daughter."

Cameron smiled again, his eyes lingering on Nicole. "That's awesome. You've got yourself one heck of a teacher, Nicole."

"Don't I know it." She made a face and brushed off her jacket. "Thanks for checking in."

"Just doing my rounds. It was really nice to meet you both. Stay safe out there on these...harrowing trails." He gave her a wink.

With a nod to Jack, he pushed off and disappeared.

"Well, he was friendly," Jack said.

"And a fan of yours, apparently," she said with a wry smile.

But he didn't smile back, he just searched her face, no doubt waiting for her to change her mind. She wasn't going to. She didn't want to do this.

"It's okay," he finally said.

"Is it?"

"You kept your part of the bargain." He gestured toward her skis and poles. "You're out here. You tried. You did it. That was all I asked."

It wasn't all he'd asked—well, it certainly wasn't all he wanted. He wanted her to ski...but there were too many memories and the best way to avoid them was to stay off this mountain. Forever.

"Can I have hot chocolate now, Daddy?" she asked, purposely keeping her voice childish and light.

He laughed. "How you end every ski day, Nic. With extra marshmallows." He gave her a hug. "Absolutely, honey. Whatever you want."

What she wanted was...to not disappoint Jack Kessler. She wanted to capture this moment and conquer this mountain and ski with her father until he couldn't ski anymore.

But that, it seemed, was not meant to be.

Chapter Eight

The morning started like any other at Snowberry Lodge—except, of course, for the part where Cindy's ex-husband had arrived on the property two days ago and casually strolled into her life again like it hadn't been a decade since he left.

She sat at the organized chaos that was her desk, peering over a spreadsheet splayed across the computer screen. She clutched a pen in one hand and a coffee cup in the other.

Something was sidetracking her concentration, though. Was it the aroma of MJ's cinnamon pecan waffles wafting from the kitchen around the corner, or the fact that Jack was back? Both were equally distracting. And... tempting.

Sighing audibly, she leaned back and closed her eyes, letting all the emotions hit her. Jack Kessler—the only man she'd ever really loved, the man she'd married, shared a life with, had a child with, and divorced after twenty years—was currently in Cabin One.

She could hardly believe it, and she had no idea which of her feelings to grab onto and lasso into submission. Shock at the sight of him? Age-old anger at how their marriage crumbled for reasons she could barely remember? Frustration that she needed him to get out of her financial bind?

Nah, none of those really bothered her.

It was a different kind of emotion that gripped her throat and made it hard to swallow coffee...and the truth. The ache in her heart when she looked at him, the memories, the laughter, the nights, and unity that came with sharing a last name and a bed for twenty long years.

The last thing she needed was to fall back in love with Jack. Or acknowledge that she'd never fallen out of love with him, despite telling everyone—including herself—that she had.

But the *first* thing she needed? She squinted at the bottom line on the spreadsheet. December income and, like it or not, Jack could most certainly help with that.

She'd been stunned that Nicole had extended the invitation, but they'd all agreed to do whatever they could to make these numbers work. The idea was brilliant because Jack created magic in the form of Christmas sleigh rides, and those sleigh rides brought in good money, plenty of attention, and booked rooms.

So, Jack? Well, yeah. It was tough, but if it helped with the goal of a solid December, she'd grin and bear it. In fact, she should be as nice to him as possible, considering the magnitude of the favor he was doing for them.

She tapped her finger against the mug and let her gaze slide to the window...in the direction of the closest cabin on the property, where Jack was right now.

She felt pulled to visit him, but surely he'd be over

here for breakfast soon. In the meantime, she had to make sense of the numbers and be prepared for her next conversation with Henry Lassiter.

If she went ahead and decided to give Henry a very small percentage of the business, it would take them through the next couple of years and the renovations they so desperately needed to do.

If that fell through, they still had to pay that tax bill. Everyone was doing their share to solve that problem. Jack would do sleigh rides, Red had agreed to put that Santa suit on for one more year, Gracie was talking up the lodge, Nic was running a huge sale, and MJ was—

"You're doing that thing again."

She whipped around. MJ was standing in her doorway, pointing at her with a spatula, her blue eyes twinkling.

"What thing?" Cindy's gaze dropped over her sister's slightly splattered apron with the Snowberry Lodge logo embroidered on the front.

"The thing where you stare at a spreadsheet like it's going to transform into different numbers if you glare hard enough."

Cindy groaned. "Is it that obvious?"

MJ shrugged. "I know you better than anyone. Which is why I saved enough batter to make you two waffles. You want?"

"More than life itself." She pushed up, then hesitated. "Did Jack come in for breakfast yet?"

"It's seven in the morning. Have you met Jack Kessler?"

She nodded, then cocked her head. "But he's on East Coast time, so I bet he's up. Why don't you make those waffles for him, and I'll take them over. I've had two people message us about sleigh rides, so we really should talk about a schedule. Also, we're not paying him, so let's feed him well."

"Good call."

Cindy followed her sister into the sun-warmed kitchen, leaning against the counter to watch MJ pour the batter into the waffle iron. Their few guests were in the dining area, chatting and enjoying a spectacular breakfast.

"So? Dare I ask the obvious?" MJ looked up with a sly smile.

"Does he want extra syrup?"

MJ laughed. "Come on, little sister. Truth. How do you feel about this surprise guest?"

Cindy hesitated, taking a sip of the cold coffee she brought with her, then putting the cup in the sink. The move bought her a little time to gather her thoughts.

"It was a shock," she said. "And weird, though not in a bad way. A good weird, if that makes sense. Almost like he never left, which is just bizarre." Of course, it had been Christmastime when they'd said their official goodbye.

She'd seen him a few times after that—when Nic graduated from college, and he'd come after Mom passed away. But it was that last Christmas that haunted her memories, a time so much like this one.

"He looks good," MJ mused.

"Mmm." Had Jack ever *not* looked good? She remembered the day he'd come in to interview for a job at Snowberry—also during the holidays—and her father hired him to run the sleighs. He'd been off the skiing circuit for a year after getting injured and needed a little supplemental income until he could heal enough to give ski lessons.

She'd heard of him, of course—everyone in Park City knew Flying Jack—but she'd never met him until that day. She'd walked into the very office that she'd just left, and Red introduced her to their new sleigh driver.

It might not have been love at first sight, but it was a big, bad, juicy crush that she was happy to say went both ways.

"So how does that make you feel?" MJ pressed, oblivious to Cindy's little march down memory lane.

She sighed. "I don't know what to feel, MJ. I haven't seen him in years, and now he's back, talking about sleigh rides and laughing with Nicole like nothing has changed. It's strange."

"Do you think you'll spend time together or just sort of exist around each other?"

"I don't know," she admitted. "I don't hate him, you know. I've long ago forgiven him for his choice."

"Does he know that?" MJ asked.

"I guess." Cindy lifted a shoulder. "I don't know. Maybe Nicole has told him but, honestly, I don't know."

"You should tell him."

She studied her sister's precise moves as she sliced up

some fruit and deftly poured syrup into a small white pitcher.

"Maybe," Cindy said, unconvinced. "But why?"

"Because..." MJ grabbed a wooden tray and set up a breakfast serving with silverware, a glass of juice, a steaming cup of coffee, that syrup, a pat of butter, and a little tiny flower in a vase. "He should know that."

"Why?" Cindy asked again.

Lifting the waffle iron to reveal perfectly golden, fluffy waffles, she used tongs to place them at a playful angle on a plate, garnished with the sliced fruit, then tapped her powdered sugar like snow all over them.

"Because I think there's still something there."

Cindy choked. "Excuse me?"

"I watched him at dinner last night, and the night he got here. He looked at you, only you, then you some more." She finished the tray and swept her hand over it like a proud magician. "I dare the Grand Stinking Hyatt to do better," she said.

"They can't." Cindy stepped to the mudroom to get her jacket. "He really...looked at me?"

"Gazed, I would say. With longing and...another word that begins with L and rhymes with...glove."

"Shut up." Cindy slipped into the sleeves. "I'll take breakfast to him and hope he considers it payment for his services."

"You can always add a hug," she said. "I don't think he'd mind."

Cindy rolled her eyes and reached for the tray. "This looks so good, MJ."

Her sister leaned in, and Cindy waited for another comment about how no other hotel could rival her work.

"Ten years doesn't erase the kind of love you two had," she whispered, making Cindy startle at the statement. "I mean it, Cin. In its day, it was a beautiful thing. Almost as good as George and me."

Could she be right? "Ten years and one big divorce most certainly does erase it," she said in her most pragmatic voice, hoping to stomp out the hope that crawled up her chest.

She couldn't fall for Jack again. She couldn't.

"Thanks for the waffles," she said. "And the really lame advice."

MJ snorted a laugh and put a stainless-steel cloche on top of the waffles. "Quick, go before they get cold. He'll want the butter to melt when he slathers it on."

"The butter, yes," Cindy said, walking to the door, then looking over her shoulder. "But not me."

HER BOOTS SLID a little on the snow as Cindy made the walk to Cabin One, which sat on the crest of a hill about a hundred yards from the back of the lodge. Despite being the smallest of their "studio" cabins with just a bedroom, living area and kitchenette, it had always been one of her favorites. It didn't have the mountain view that some of the others had, but it was cozy and rustic. It had a quaint porch that was a dream in the summer and a stone fireplace that dominated the room and made for delightful winter sleeping.

This close to Christmas, the wooden railing was trimmed in garlands and lights, the planks dusted with fresh snow. As she approached, she felt her heart rate pick up.

Dang it, Cin. Why are you nervous? It was Jack, for heaven's sake.

Yeah. That's why she was nervous.

She knocked twice before the door creaked open.

He was barefoot in plaid sleep pants and a white T-shirt, mug in hand, hair tousled and eyes sleepy.

"Hey," he said, voice gravelly from sleep, then his gaze dropped to the tray. "Room service? I don't remember Snowberry offering that."

She shrugged. "We feel sorry that you aren't getting paid."

"I'm not?" he asked with a sly smile. "Nic totally duped me."

She laughed. "You will accept MJ's culinary delights and be happy."

Taking the tray from her, he took a deep inhale. "I'm already overpaid. Come on in," he said, kicking the door wider and leaning his head toward the warmth of the cabin. "If I know your sister, there's more than enough for two here."

She hesitated, not sure what to do.

"Come on, Cin. Let's catch up. I made a fire."

She tapped the snow off her boots and slipped them

off just inside the door, the bold aroma of fresh coffee mixing with the smoky pine in the fireplace.

His bed was made—sort of—and she could still see the imprint of his head on his pillow, reminding her that he always slept on his back. Always. He never turned all night, except to cuddle her.

Funny the things you know about your own husband.

He put the tray on the small two-top table near the kitchenette, grabbing a mug from a rack on the counter.

"Two sugars and no cream?" he asked.

"Nothing has changed."

He poured the mug and grabbed two packets of sugar, putting them on the table and inviting her to sit down.

"Well, a lot of things have changed," he said. "The ski shed's been painted. The town has grown. And our daughter gets more beautiful and grown up every day."

She smiled and met his gaze as she sat down. "That she does," she agreed. "She told me skiing was, uh, challenging."

"She's still terrified."

Cindy nodded, stirring in the sugar. "The fact that you got her out there at all was a shocker to me."

"It was part of our deal—for me to come, I mean."

Her heart dropped a little. "You needed to make a deal?"

"I'd have come without a deal," he said as he took the warming dome off the waffles and made the appropriate cooing sounds at the sight and smell of MJ's masterpiece breakfast. "I wanted to help. I thought she could conquer that fear and ski again. Now, I'm not so sure."

Cindy sighed, sipping the hot coffee and looking at the crackling fire.

Jack poured some syrup over the waffles and lifted his fork, offering it to her. "Share?"

The intimate gesture made her heart flip. "I'm good, thanks. I wanted to talk about the sleigh rides," she said, hoping her voice didn't sound as tense as she felt. "I'm getting inquiries."

"Let's get them up and running," he said, taking a bite. "And deliver that Snowberry magic."

She lifted the hot coffee and blew on the steam gently. "You think you can bring it back?"

"Hey." He leaned back in the chair and ran a hand over his silver temple. "I might be ten years older and a bit more gray than the last time I did a Snowberry sleigh ride, but I can hold the reins, handle the hills, and take everyone's breath away. Benny found the old carriage driver outfit, too, which always...slays." He winked as he took a bite. "Sorry," he added with his mouth full.

She tried to laugh, but she just sat like a fool drinking in the sight of him and getting a little tipsy from it.

"You okay, Cindy?" he asked after he swallowed and dabbed his mouth with a napkin as if he might have drib-bled syrup.

She had to get it together around him, so she slid right to her happy place: work.

"Yes, I'm fine. I've spent the morning wrestling with

finances and, I can confirm, we're on shaky ground. I'm hoping the sleigh rides will be enough to get our December bookings increased, but...who knows about next year? And the year after that? I just can't see a good way out."

Jack winced as he cut into the waffle. "I hate that it got this bad."

"It's tough these days, as you know."

"I should have..." He sighed and looked away. "You know, I'm just going to say this, okay? I want to get it out there."

Her heart stuttered at the serious tone. "What's that?"

"I'm sorry for leaving," he said, turning back to meet her gaze. "I'm sorry I put work over you and Nic and...us. I know why I did it, but that doesn't make it right. I don't know. I just want you to know I regret it every day and I believe I owe you an apology now that ten years has passed."

Cindy searched his face, a little breathless, but so touched by the apology, remembering MJ's words. He'd never made an official apology before, but then, they hadn't had an acrimonious divorce. Just a painful one.

"We made the best decisions we could at the time," she said, lowering her voice to a meaningful whisper. "Jack, I promise, I forgave you a long time ago."

His dark eyes flickered. "You did?"

She nodded. "And the apology should go both ways. I'm sorry I threw in the towel so easily. I should have... waited it out. You did retire from ESPN eventually. I maybe should have...tried harder. And not put this place at the top of my priority list."

His eyes shuttered. "God knows I've forgiven you for that long ago."

God might know that, but Cindy hadn't. The words were like a balm on her heart. "Obviously, since you gave up your Christmas to come here."

He lifted a shoulder. "Not much to give up. I'm... alone."

She was more surprised by the tone than the love-life update.

"Unless you count Bertie," he added with a chuckle. "But my mother has little time for me these days. She's the most popular octogenarian at the retirement community. Now, *she* has a social life. I have...skiing in winter, hiking in summer, and...not a whole lot else."

Her heart dipped. "Are you lonely, Jack?"

She expected a joke but got a sad smile. "I'm fine, Cindy. It's just not the life I pictured at sixty. I travel, I do some consulting work and lessons, and I keep an eye on Bertie when she lets me. But..." He swallowed. "Let's just say, it's nice to be back here and have a purpose. And it's really nice to see you looking so good and happy."

Did she look good and happy? "More like overworked and worried."

He put his hand over hers, the touch warm and unexpectedly nice. "Then why don't you take a sleigh ride with me today? I need to practice the trails. Is the creek running or frozen? Is the path to Aspen View open? I need to relearn my way around...Snowberry."

Or around her?

The thought made her heart flip, or maybe that was the familiar and wonderful feeling of her husband's touch.

"Well," she finally said. "We need a horse."

Jack looked surprised. "We have a horse. Nic took me to see Copper yesterday and he's still a beauty. A little finicky, but he's still got it. Probably."

Cindy arched a dubious brow as she took a deep drink of coffee. "You want to test that theory? Nic is blinded by her love for the horse, but Copper is a total diva. He does *not* want to pull a sleigh."

"He's a horse. He was born for this." Jack grinned, finishing up the plate of waffles and popping a few grapes in his mouth. "Come on, I'm ready to roll. Well, glide."

"I'll take your tray back while you dress. Meet you at the stable in ten minutes."

MJ was not in the kitchen when Cindy dropped the tray off, so she headed straight back to the stable, meeting Jack coming from his cabin as she got to the oversized door. He wore jeans and boots, and a black puffer vest that was a stark contrast to the silver in his hair.

Smiling at her, he pushed the door open, and they stepped onto the hay-covered wooden floor, instantly greeted by Copper's familiar neigh.

"Hey, boy," Jack said softly as he approached the stall and met the horse's big brown eyes.

"He's a sweet guy," Cindy said, watching Jack's strong hands stroke Copper's head. "Until he's a drama king, which does happen."

Jack smiled. "You going to let her call you a drama king, Copper-man?"

Copper flicked his ears and whinnied.

"I remember when we picked him for Nic," Jack said, turning to her. "We went out to that farm in Herriman. We could see the copper mine on the western mountains and that's how you picked the name."

"I do remember." She also remembered the tension in the car and the fact that they knew this horse was more than a replacement for Whistler. He was a way to ease Nicole's pain when they told her they were splitting up. "That farm's gone," she said, not wanting to think of those dark days. "Herriman is a beautiful upscale suburb of Salt Lake City now."

"Ah, progress." He reached into a bag next to the stall, grabbing a peppermint. "You ready to take a ride on the sleigh, big fella? I guess you do more work than ride, but I'll go easy on you, I promise."

He held out the peppermint that Copper slurped up, opening the latch to guide him out.

"You get him comfortable, Cin," Jack said. "I'll get the equipment."

Copper was a little tense when Jack went to the storage cabinet and pulled out the harness, so Cindy walked him outside to the paddock, offering peppermints as they strolled.

A few minutes later, Jack had dragged everything to the sleigh and hustled back up the hill to the paddock.

Copper watched warily, but let them lead him out, down the path, and right to the sleigh that sat outside the ski shed. Jack had laid out the equipment. He walked ahead, picking up the padded collar and traces to buckle them together, inspecting each piece for wear.

"You remember how to do this?" Cindy asked as she and the horse got closer.

With each step, Copper's hesitancy grew more obvious as he whinnied and kicked at the snow.

"I could do this in my sleep. Bring him closer?"

She tried but Copper stayed planted in place.

"Except Whistler was a bit more obedient," Jack said, looping the bellyband. "Want to hook up the breeching?"

While Copper watched from a few feet away, they worked side by side, adjusting straps, brushing off snow, laughing as they fumbled with frozen buckles. They'd done this a million times together, Cindy thought, using muscle memory to finish the task.

Once everything was prepped, Jack began slipping the padded collar over Copper's head. The horse resisted immediately, backing up.

"Don't go all diva now," Jack said. "This is your job."

Copper let out a loud, indignant snort.

Cindy laughed and grabbed a peppermint from her coat pocket and offered it with a coaxing smile. "There you go, buddy."

Copper took the mint—and then stepped on Jack's boot.

"Ow! Okay, now it's personal."

It took several tries to get the collar on, and even longer to fasten the traces to the singletree. Copper refused to stand still. He nibbled Jack's coat, tried to back away, and at one point nearly sat down.

Despite the cold, Jack wiped sweat from his brow. "He's like a puppy. How much does Nicole baby this guy?"

"Quite a bit." Cindy shook her head, patting the horse's long, soft snout.

Finally, after what felt like a barnyard comedy routine, Copper stood mostly still in front of the sleigh, the harness secured. Jack stepped back to admire their work.

"We did it," he said.

Cindy tilted her head. "Almost. You want to test the pull?"

Jack climbed up and took the reins. "Let's see what you got, Copper."

Copper took one tentative step forward, then stopped. Then another. Then—nothing.

"Come on, Cin." Jack reached his hand down. "He might want a passenger."

Doubtful of that, she put her foot on the runner and took his hand, letting him ease her up to the leather bench perched high behind Copper.

"All right, here we—"

Copper bolted sideways, making the sleigh lurch off-kilter in the snow. Jack shouted, Cindy shrieked and grabbed him, both of them nearly sliding out as the whole apparatus tipped dangerously close to its side.

Jack was completely pressed against her, his face an

inch from hers, the pressure and warmth pinning her in place.

Moving meant risking tipping the sleigh completely, but they couldn't stay like this forever...or could they?

"This horse," he said softly into her ear, "has officially gotten the better of us."

"Just pray he doesn't take off, 'cause we'd be dead."

His eyes shuttered as he let his cheek touch hers. "Not a bad way to go, Cinnie."

The old nickname whispered so intimately had her as off kilter as the sleigh. "Jack."

"Yeah."

"We gotta get out of this sleigh."

"Or we could..."

He didn't finish, but held her gaze, so close she could see the flecks of gold in his dark chocolate eyes. She could even count his lashes, which were still thick and long and one of the many beautiful things about his face.

Wait a second. What was she doing? Falling for Jack Kessler? He'd been here two days and they were hanging off the side of the sleigh, about to kiss?

This had to—

"I can't watch this anymore." Nicole burst out the front door of the ski shed. "You two are killing me."

They laughed and moved enough for Jack to lift his weight and free Cindy. Nicole marched over and pushed the sleigh back into position, giving them a strange look.

"What are you guys trying to do?"

Good question, Cindy thought. What *were* they trying to do? Rekindle a long-dead romance?

Just so she could wave goodbye to Jack yet again when he jetted off for Vermont?

No. No. *No.*

She managed to climb out of the sleigh and brush off her jacket and jeans, rooting for dignity.

"That horse is...not going to do the job," she said. "Should I go start researching one we could board for the month of December?"

"No," Nicole and Jack said the word at exactly the same time in their same tone of relentless determination.

"We'll train him," Jack said.

"I'll work with him," Nicole added. "The fact that you got him this far is huge."

"And then we can take that ride, Cin," Jack added.

Cindy took a step back, holding up her hands. "I've had enough brushes with, um, danger for one day. I'll go back to the safety of my spreadsheets. Good luck, you two."

With a quick smile and an awkward wave, she stepped away, trying not to rush into the sanctuary of her office. There, she could breathe again and talk herself out of these...feelings.

Jack was her weakness, and she couldn't let herself get hurt again. That would just be foolish.

Chapter Nine
Nicole

Copper snorted so hard his bridle jingled.

Nicole braced her boots in the snowbank beside the sleigh, one gloved hand resting on Copper's flank.

"You're making me look bad, bud," she murmured, stroking the mane of the horse she'd fed, brushed, and coddled for a decade, who now stood rooted to the snowy ground like an overgrown lawn ornament.

Her father, seated up on the sleigh bench, gave the reins a gentle twitch. "He's stubborn today."

Nicole shot him a look. "He's stubborn every day."

She rubbed Copper's neck, feeling the powerful muscles coiled tight beneath his mahogany-colored coat. He wasn't scared, exactly. Just...unwilling. Like something inside him remembered what had happened the last time he tried to pull the sleigh and said...*Nope. Not again.*

Something had startled him the first time he pulled the sleigh—maybe a loud noise. He hated ski helicopters and the rare rumble of thunder. Whatever it had been, he'd stumbled off the trail and, since that day, he hated the very sight of this thing.

"Baby, I get it," she whispered into his ear, getting a noisy shake in response.

Boy, did she get it. She knew what "spooked" felt like, what the sight—or sound—of something scary could do to you. She knew how an ordeal remained engraved on your memory and paralyzed a person. Or a horse.

They'd always been connected on so many levels, whether Nicole was saddled up and trotting over the trails of Snowberry with him or just lazing in the paddock. They spoke the same language and Copper truly understood English.

When he wanted to.

As she coaxed him forward, she remembered the moment that had her frozen in shock just a few minutes earlier. Brianna had seen what was going on out here and had waved Nicole to the window.

Like bad little kids spying on their parents, the two of them had peered out and observed the whole sweet and, yes, romantic scene. They'd giggled and poked each other and laughed...but something about the encounter hadn't really been funny.

It had been...dreamy.

Was there any chance? Maybe. She'd seen the way Dad had leaned closer, the way Mom had let his cheek brush hers. What had he said to her? An old memory? A dear name? An inside joke?

They had so much history. They should—

"You gonna try to move this horse, Nic, or are we going to give sleigh sits instead of sleigh rides?"

She threw a look over her shoulder at her father, half tempted to tell him what was on her mind. But that might jinx it. That might make him go running off back to Vermont.

"I'm trying," she insisted, wrapping her arm around Copper's neck. "I'm bonding with him. It takes a minute."

"And a peppermint," he suggested.

"Good thought." She reached in her pocket and grabbed a candy to hold under Copper's nose. His ears twitched. His lips wiggled. He didn't move. "But apparently, he can't be bribed. I have to talk to him."

"All right. You work your magic."

Cooing into his ear, she stroked his mane over and over, watching the fight slip from his eyes. "All right, big guy. Eyes ahead," she said softly. "Where you look is where you go."

Jack chuckled behind her. "And where'd you learn that line?"

"From the master," she joked. "Come on, Copper. Come on, baby." She urged him forward, and he took one small step, enough to jingle the bells attached to his harness.

And he froze again.

"Do sleigh bells scare him?" Jack asked.

"They remind him of the first time you harnessed him to this thing." She turned and looked at him. "You remember? It was your last Christmas here and I was home from college."

He nodded. "Of course. He slipped out where the

trail turns into Moose Creek and there's that big drop at the east end of the meadow."

"He'll ride past that in the summer," Nicole said. "But he hates that trail in the winter, not that I take him out much in this weather."

"I used to practice skiing down that drop," her father mused, making her wince at the idea.

She gave the horse a kiss to cover. "We need you to fight through the winter blues, Copper. We need sleigh rides. Without you, we can't make December and if we don't make December..." She pressed her lips to his ear. "You'll be boarded somewhere, and no one will be happy."

He took one step.

"There you go, there," she said encouragingly. "Let's try it again."

She tugged his bridle and stepped forward slowly. One step. Another. Copper watched her, his massive hooves unmoving.

"C'mon," she coaxed. "Weight on your downhill foot."

Jack laughed again. "At least you were listening yesterday."

"Not as well as he is," she crooned to Copper. "Now do better than I did, big boy. Another step. And another."

He did, making the bells jingle softly, but he ignored it, clearly mesmerized by Nicole's voice.

Copper licked his lips. Nicole placed the peppermint on her palm and held it out again. "What else do you say on that mountain, Dad?"

"Trust your body," he answered. "It knows what to do. Pick a line and follow. Eyes ahead, not at your feet. Focus, focus."

She raised a hand to thank him, repeating all the words to her horse. Slow, soft, with the same loving tone her father had used with her on the slopes. For a few beats, Copper stayed very still, then a single hoof shifted.

Nicole exhaled. "That's it. Good boy. Trust yourself, baby. Just..." She threw a look at Dad.

"Trust your body," he said. "Trust the snow. Trust the skis."

She laughed softly. "Trust the sleigh," she said instead. "Go with the rhythm. Follow, follow, here you go..."

She stepped forward, keeping an even pace with the horse's shoulder. The harness creaked as Copper slowly leaned into it.

"You want this," she murmured, remembering back years to her own training. Before she deeply feared snow and skis and being buried alive. "You *know* you want this, Copper. Steady...steady..."

Copper's hooves crunched forward in the snow, dragging the sleigh with a soft groan of iron runners.

"We're moving!" Dad said in a loud whisper, as if any actual noise could bring it all to a stop.

Nicole smiled wide, warmth flooding her chest. "That's my boy. You're doing it."

Copper let out a soft nicker, his tail swishing. One slow step turned into two. Then three. Nicole kept alongside him, whispering praise, offering the occasional peppermint reward.

They reached the curve of the drive just as Red appeared, stomping through the snow like a mountain king.

He stopped short, his bushy brows shooting up as he rubbed his bald head. "Well, I'll be. Is that Copper pulling that sleigh?"

Jack waved a gloved hand. "Sure is. Nic got him going."

Red clapped his hands together. "Hot diggity dog, Nicky. Nice work. Mind if I hop on?"

Nicole stepped back, still grinning. "Be my guest. I've got to get back to work anyway. Think you can do this without me?"

Jack tilted his head. "Not as well, but we'll try." He added that Jack Kessler smile that she knew so well. The one that used to greet her at the bottom of every hill, the one that oozed pride and support and love. She loved that smile.

"Well done, young lady," he said with a wink.

She nodded, her throat thick with how much she loved and missed her father, and how supportive he'd been her whole life. Had he been disappointed that she'd quit skiing? Yes, but he never stopped being an amazing father.

"Have fun," she said, her voice taut. "And be careful!"

"We got this, girlie," Red assured her as he climbed aboard with a grunt and a creak.

Copper huffed, then started moving again, now with confidence. Nicole stood in the snowy path, watching as her horse pulled the sleigh deeper into the property, past the paddock, and toward the row of cabins.

Well done, indeed. As she watched the back of the sleigh disappear over the rise, her eyes burned, and one thought danced in her head.

If Copper could do it...

Could she? She turned on her heel and jogged down the path, determination sparking in her chest. If she stopped and second-guessed this decision, it would be all over. She had to do this.

With a burst of excitement, she threw the door of the ski shed open, practically colliding with some customers carrying bags and poles.

"Oh, sorry! And thank you! Come again! Have fun on the slopes!" She gave them a wave and met Brianna's surprised look from behind the counter.

"You got him going?" she asked.

"I did...and it got me going."

Brianna's brows lifted. "How so?"

She caught her breath from the run, placing both hands on the counter and leaning in. "I want to try again."

Brianna blinked. "You do?"

God bless her bestie—she didn't have to ask what Nicole wanted to try.

"I do," she said. "I want to get over this thing. Will you take me?"

"Yes. Yes! Of course I will. First lift at Deer Valley. Are you sure me and not your dad?"

Nicole nodded fiercely. "Yes. I think he might accidentally hit some triggers for me, but if I go with you..."

"No triggers," she promised, coming around the counter to offer a huge hug. "I'm proud of you."

"Don't be yet." Nicole laughed into her shoulder, hugging back. "But we have to get someone to cover the store or go really, really early."

"I vote for early, and we'll get coverage. Maybe enough to stay for a few extra runs."

Nicole sighed. "That would be so nice. I want to..." She bit her lip. "I want to ski so bad, Bri."

"Then ski you shall!" She gave her another squeeze, then spun them both around toward the jacket rack. "And I say you do it in style." She grabbed a bubblegum-pink ski jacket and held it up. "This. Absolutely this."

Nicole wrinkled her nose. "That looks like cotton candy."

"Exactly. It screams, 'I am joyful and fearless and *adorable* on skis.'"

Nicole took the jacket. "Okay. Fine. And when I wipe out, I will look like a massive Pepto-Bismol spill."

"*If* you wipe out," Bri corrected. "I'm a very good instructor."

They shared a grin. Then Bri gave her a sly look. "So, what exactly was going on with Jack and Cindy on the sleigh? I could have sworn they kissed."

Nicole just shook her head, smiling. "Right? I couldn't tell, but Mom was a tad flustered, and Dad looked…" She let out a moan. "I don't know. I hate that I want them to rediscover each other but, oh, man, do I ever."

"Same," Bri said. "And just to give you a little more motivation? If you start skiing again, your dad will have another reason to stick around Park City."

Nicole looked down at the jacket in her hands, letting her imagination go there and ache for how much she wanted that, too. "I'm doing it, Bri. I swear, I'm doing it."

And just like Copper, she'd find her way forward. One slow, steady, peppermint-sweet step at a time.

Chapter Ten

Red

The sleigh creaked under his weight as Red settled onto the bench beside Jack, who already had the reins in his hands and a look of calm focus on his face. Copper gave a faint whinny ahead of them, his hooves shifting in the snow. The big Belgian Draft horse looked surprised to be attached to the sleigh but had—somehow, with Nicole's help—gotten himself moving.

Red still wasn't sure if it was a Christmas miracle or sheer dumb luck.

Jack glanced over. "Ready?"

Red grunted. "As long as I don't have to put that itchy jacket on and pretend to like kids, I'll ride this thing all day."

"You don't like being Santa, Red?"

"I'm over it, as the kids say. Too old, too tired, too... well, I guess you can't be too fat to be Santa."

"You're not any of those things." Jack clicked his tongue and gave the reins a tug. Copper took a few tentative steps, then found his rhythm. "You're Grumpy Santa, king of social media."

Red snorted. "I don't quite get why, but it's working,"

he said. "Benny told me this morning we have another thousand followers."

"And no one knows yet? Not Cindy or MJ?"

Red held up his hand. "Let's keep it that way, Jack. The kid wants a dog so bad for Christmas, and he's sure that his mom will be furious at him—and me—for playing with the phone. She's adamant about him not having one of those things, or access to mine."

"That's strict," Jack noted.

"She's a single mother," Red said, rising to his grand-daughter's defense. "She has to be strict. Benny knows if he strays too far from the rules, it'll cost him his doggo."

"Then maybe he shouldn't be on social media accruing thousands of followers," Jack said with a wry smile.

"Maybe not. But we're in a bind so bad that you left... whatever it is you have in Vermont and flew here to run this sleigh."

Jack slid him a look, not answering.

"And I," Red continued, "agreed to put that stupid jacket on once more and promise to give kids toys they might not ever get."

That made Jack smile while Red leaned back, sparing a glance at one of the cabins, seeing a lone gentleman step outside Cabin Five and raise his hand in greeting.

"We're all doing something, taking a risk, upsettin' our lives—all for Snowberry Lodge."

"That's true," Jack agreed.

"So's Benny. We'll come clean on Christmas morning —right about the time he's holding a new puppy."

"I get it," Jack said. "The secret is safe."

Copper slowed again, but Jack flicked the reins, and the horse picked up the pace, pulling the sleigh around the bend of the last cabin, headed toward the open trail that curved behind the property.

"This place looks great," Jack observed, squinting into the bright winter sun bouncing off the snow.

"*Nature* looks great," Red corrected as they came around the long drive to the house where he lived with Gracie and Benny. "The place is...old, like I am."

"Looks pretty good to me," Jack said.

Red tried to see his home of eighty-two years through another man's eyes, and he had to admit, it did look like a fine place.

The rolling hills around Snowberry Lodge stretched wide and white in front of them, soft mounds of snow blanketing the fields and trees dusted with frost.

Of course, he knew every inch of this land. His entire life was pressed into this land—hard winters, achingly beautiful summers, the smell of pine and earth, the laughter of kids who'd grown up in the middle of Utah's breathtaking landscape.

"Vermont's pretty and all," Jack said, his gaze traveling the same path as Red's, his thoughts maybe on their own journey. "But this piece of the country is spectacular."

At the wistful note in Jack's voice, Red eyed him carefully, trying to gauge what the man was really feeling.

Red cleared his throat, not wanting to dwell on old

hurts. If Cindy could get over it, then he could, too. Plus, Jack had come to help them, and that meant something to Red. Meant a lot.

"Can't believe that horse is actually movin'," he mused, more to coax Jack into talking than state the obvious.

Jack chuckled. "Nic's got a way with the little prince. Should I head up to Pinecone Ridge?"

"I'd go where Copper leads," Red said. "As long as you're mapping out a route for the rides."

"I am," Jack said, keeping his eyes on the snowy trail ahead.

A few long beats of silence passed, with nothing but the winter wind and the soft hoofbeats, the hiss of the runners gliding over snow.

Red wasn't good at talking nonsense. MJ was the one who filled silence like a radio station. Cindy, too, when she wasn't bogged down in books and bills. But Red didn't like dancing around things, especially not with a man like Jack.

But some things had to be said between them, and now was as good a time as any.

"How's it feel to be back?" he asked, hoping that was enough to get a conversation going.

"Different," Jack replied without hesitation. "Like an outsider looking in."

"You are."

"I wasn't, once." He threw Red a look. "But being here is like I'm standing at a storefront window and wanting everything that's inside, but I can't afford a thing."

The comment really threw Red. He wasn't expecting the man to sound either nostalgic or regretful.

Red considered that, staring at the passing pine trees. "Well, this place has a way of gettin' under your skin."

"Yeah." Jack tugged on the reins as Copper veered too close to a snowbank. "I missed it. More than I realized."

Red nodded, keen on the candor. There was a time when he and Jack could talk about anything. George, too, when MJ's husband was still alive. The three of them were the men of Snowberry. Jack and George were the sons that Red never had.

George died—which was sad. But Jack left—which was dumb.

"Then why'd you leave, Jack?" he asked, the question rising up and coming right out. Oh, well. He was entitled to honesty and bluntness at his ripe old age.

Jack didn't answer right away. The jingle of the sleigh bells filled the space.

"I got a second chance at my dream," Jack said after a moment. "After my injury, I thought I was done with the world of competitive skiing—which, as you know, isn't like everyday, ordinary skiing."

"I know what it is," Red said.

"But the ESPN job? It gave me a purpose again. Made me feel like I mattered."

"You always mattered," Red muttered. "You mattered to Cindy, and to Nicole. Heck, you mattered to me. You mattered for the years you juggled this life and that one."

"I couldn't juggle anymore," he admitted gruffly. "The travel was constant. Cindy wanted me to choose and…"

And he chose ESPN and skiing and the rush of his old life. Red tried to understand—he always did—but he still had a rough time with the choice Jack had made. And Cindy's rather rushed decision to file for divorce.

"We were all crushed when you left," Red said. "I get it, I guess. But I didn't back then."

Jack turned to look at him. "I know that now, Red. I don't blame you, really. It felt like I had to choose between being somebody or staying behind and fading away." He stared straight ahead at Copper's swooshing tail as they glided forward. "I felt like I was settling for a life that was quiet and mundane, and I got this opportunity, you know? I'm not saying it was the right choice, but it was the one I made."

Red grunted. "Mundane can be good."

"I know that now," Jack whispered.

Red didn't speak while he watched a hawk circle lazily overhead.

"Cindy was heartbroken, you know," he said.

"Of course I know that. I was, too. I wished she hadn't asked me to choose—"

"And she wished you'd chosen her."

Jack winced. "I know, Red. She told me today she forgave me, and I guess it's…fine."

"Oh, she probably did forgive you. Ten years'll do

that to you. But it isn't fine." Red gave him a hard look. "She never really got *fine* after you left."

Jack's hands tightened on the reins. "*She* divorced *me*, remember?"

"Like it was yesterday," Red replied. "I always thought she jumped the gun a bit on that one, but you know Cindy. She's a fixer. Sometimes her solutions are dumber than the problem. But when she's not happy with something, she's gonna change it, like it or not. Can't stop her. Nicole, too. But, whoa, the cost was high. You missed a lot, Jack. Birthdays. Snowstorms. Flat tires. Real life."

Jack's eyes shuttered as he sighed, his exhale making a little puff of fog in the crisp wintery air. "I'm sorry, Red, for whatever that's worth. Being back here has made me realize just how much of a..."

Red waited, inching closer, wondering what he was going to say.

"How much of a mistake I made." The admission came rushing out, his words picking up speed like the sleigh when Copper trotted down a small hill.

Red rubbed a hand over his face, blinking against the wind that stung his eyes—well, something stung them.

"Jack," he said on a gruff whisper. "I held a grudge. I'll own up to it. You were like a son to me. I was proud of you. Proud you loved my daughter, proud of the family you two made. Then it was all over."

Jack didn't defend himself.

Red looked over again. "But I get it. Took me eighty years to figure it out, but sometimes a man screws up for what he thinks is the right reason. Doesn't mean he wanted to hurt anyone. Just means he was trying to find his own way."

Jack swallowed, pulling the reins gently as if he was the one trying to find his way.

"You could always stay," Red said plainly.

Jack whipped around. "Here?"

"We need a young man at this place."

"Young?" Jack laughed. "I'm sixty."

"We'll, I'm eighty-two and Benny's ten. You could fill the hole."

Jack was quiet just long enough for Red to know he was actually thinking about it, and the amount of hope that gave him should be illegal.

Finally, Jack shook his head. "It's not that simple."

"Sure it is," Red said. "The true mark of a man isn't never messing up. It's being able to admit when he has. And fixing it."

"After ten years?"

Red shrugged. "Time's all you got, son. I say make things right, while there's still time. Tell people you love them when they're right in front of you. 'Cause one day..." He swallowed a lump in his throat, running a hand through the thick of his beard, thinking of Cora, of course. But also, his parents, and George, his other son-in-law. "They're not right in front of you anymore."

Jack turned for a moment, giving Red an expression that he could tell was genuine sympathy. "You've lost some good people in your life, Red."

"But I had 'em, and that's what counts." Red cleared

his throat, adjusting against the sleigh seat, which was killing his old back. "Cora's here in spirit, I think. And I see her in my girls, all the time."

As they reached Pinecone Ridge, Copper slowed, and Jack expertly turned him at the wide part of the path. "Let's head back," he said, "before they send a search party for us."

Red chuckled at that, closing his eyes and lifting his old face to the sun as they plodded along. What needed to be said had been said, and Red could relax and enjoy the ride.

When they neared the lodge, he felt Jack tense as he elbowed Red to be sure he was awake.

"Hey, Red. You awake?"

"Barely."

"I have a question, and I need you to be honest."

"Don't know any other way," Red said. "What is it?"

"You really think I could fix things? After all this time?"

Red huffed out a breath. "Well, it sure isn't up to me, son. But I think Cindy's heart never stopped lookin' for you. Even if her head gave up."

Jack gave a short laugh. "You make it sound easy."

Red shrugged. "Nothing about life is easy. But, Jack, this one ain't that hard."

The sleigh glided past the drive to his house where a whole bunch of winter-bare apple trees looked like tall sticks in the ground. But that wasn't what Red saw.

He saw spring leaves and summer blossoms and a harvest in the fall. He could see his late wife standing there, wearing that blue flowered frock that fluttered when she walked, an apple basket on her hip. Cindy and MJ were hangin' out of the trees, calling, "Daddy, Daddy!"

"The days slip by so fast," he said, his voice thick, but he didn't care. "Don't waste them, son. That's the biggest sin you can commit."

Jack turned to him, his own eyes a little misty. "Good advice, Red. You always give good advice."

That made Red smile. "Yeah. Now get me to the kitchen before MJ tosses the waffle batter. I never got breakfast."

"Trust me, it's worth the wait," Jack said.

"Most of life is," Red replied, looking out at the trail that looped back toward the lodge.

Smoke curled from the chimney and sunlight bounced off the second-story windows. Red looked at it— at the home he'd built with his hands and his heart—and knew deep in his bones that maybe Jack Kessler wasn't done with Snowberry after all.

"Well," Red muttered, rubbing his knees, "better get used to this again if I'm gonna be stuck in that red suit for the next few weeks."

Jack grinned. "Can't do sleigh rides without Santa."

Red rolled his eyes. "Tell that to my aching back."

But his smile lingered as Copper slowed at the paddock and neighed for peppermints and praise.

Chapter Eleven

Cindy

I t had been nearly a week since Jack arrived and the sleigh rides started—not that Cindy tracked time by the comings and goings of Jack Kessler—but she had to admit, things were looking up a tiny bit.

Cautiously optimistic, she clicked through her accounting files and did some mental math.

Yes, reservations had come in. Not piles of them, but they'd barely had a chance to advertise the sleigh rides. Somehow, word got out, though.

Gracie was talking the rides up to all her customers at Sugarfall, which helped. Nicole had persuaded darn near every person who walked into the shed to book a ride, and they did. Then Cindy had updated the Snowberry website with the cutest picture of Red in full Santa gear and Jack in his Victorian costume, holding the reins of the sleigh.

That resulted in three of the cabins booking out, and several of the suites in the lodge. Not for the entire month, but it was a start. Still, they were a long way from what they needed to pay that tax bill in the new year.

And that took her back to the notes on her desk, made during yesterday's call with Henry Lassiter. The fact was, he was starting to make sense, and the next natural step would be to talk to MJ about it.

She hadn't yet, mostly because she wasn't sure she completely understood the structure of Henry's proposal. He owed her more information and she'd promised him she'd bring it up with her sister.

How would MJ react to the idea of giving up some of their ownership in order to save this place? She was reluctant to broach the subject, to be honest. They'd just had the best week—full of fun and family, long dinners and big laughs.

Cindy rubbed her temples and narrowed her eyes, her brain—and heart—shifting back to one of those dinners last night. She and Jack and MJ had lingered over decaf and cookies late into the night. Nicole and Brianna had stayed, too, after the ski shed closed, and Nina and Pedro, the couple that worked for them, had joined the fun around the table.

Benny had nodded off and needed to go to bed, so Red offered to stay with the boy—as long as Gracie brought cookies home.

They'd all talked about the mountain, the snow, Park City events, Christmas, life. They shared old stories and dear memories, and it felt like the good old days.

Because of Jack, of course.

"Oh, Jack," she whispered on a sigh that sounded as confused as she felt.

She and her ex-husband had been spending a lot of time together, giving the holidays a whole different feeling than she'd ever expected. Between planning sleigh rides, coordinating guest lists, and handling Copper's occasional stubborn streak, it all felt so right and natural.

But Cindy couldn't help wondering...were they *friends* now? Or was there something humming quietly beneath the surface? Something dangerously close to old feelings?

"Cindy Starling Kessler!" MJ called out in a sing-songy voice. "You're missing the magic! Stop working and help me decorate the big tree! I know you'll want to be sure it's perfect."

Jack and Pedro had taken a truck out to the ridge that morning to pick a gorgeous fir tree and set it up in the lodge's great room. Now, the tree was ready to be covered with Snowberry decorations. Which meant MJ would haphazardly toss her favorites in the front and Cindy would have to stealthily rehang them so they looked, well, yeah. *Perfect.*

Pushing up from her desk, Cindy abandoned the numbers and headed into the great room. She did want to make sure the tree looked good, but maybe this was her opportunity to talk with MJ about Henry Lassiter's offer.

"I thought we were waiting for Benny to get home from school," Cindy said, coming around the corner to the room where guests frequently congregated.

No one was there now, though, since they were smack dab in the middle of a great ski day.

"We are," MJ assured her. "But I thought we should get started." She leaned back, her hands on her hips as she gazed up at the deep green Douglas fir that towered toward the beamed ceiling. "She's a beauty, huh? Things are looking up, don't you think?"

Cindy nodded, following her sister's gaze to the top of the tree. "Literally."

The twelve-footer looked lovely in the rustic two-story great room at the front of Snowberry Lodge. The Christmas tree filled the spacious room with the scent of the season and looked grand next to the tall stone fireplace.

All around the room, worn but well-loved furniture—plaid armchairs, a soft caramel-hued couch, handwoven blankets—were piled with tissue-wrapped boxes and half-open storage bins filled with ornaments.

MJ, in a red cable-knit sweater and her usual messy bun, reached for an ornament and discarded it, grabbing another.

"What's wrong with that snowman?" Cindy asked.

"I'm looking for my favorites to fill up the front." She shot Cindy a look. "I know you'll tell me to spread them out, balance the color, and for the love of dear baby Jesus, don't put the homemade ones in front."

Cindy laughed. "I hate that I'm so predictable."

"You're just the only person who decorates a tree like it's a math equation," MJ teased.

"I'm organized," Cindy said in self-defense, looking into the open bin. "And you are..."

With a grin, MJ plucked out a blue glass star and hooked it on a branch, front and center. "A go-with-the-flow kind of girl," MJ finished for her. "If the star fits, hang it, I say. Who cares if it's photo worthy?"

Cindy shrugged. "Trust me, the one I have at home is not balanced or neat and have you seen Gracie's? Red and Benny went to town."

"Exactly why I thought I'd start this one before Benny gets home from school." MJ pulled out a tiny wreath made from painted dried pasta. "Remember this? Gracie made it in first grade."

Cindy came over and took the ornament in her hands, the memory softening her heart. "Even way back then she could make food into a work of art. Now, she does it with sugar and icing and has a line out the door."

MJ reached into the box again and pulled out another ornament, her eyes glinting as she hid it from Cindy. "Here's an oldie but not moldy."

"Show me."

MJ dangled the ceramic oversized engagement ring with 1995 painted on the side.

"Oh." Cindy's shoulders dropped. "The year Jack proposed. We probably should get rid of that one."

"Why?" MJ said, turning to find a branch for it. "It's part of our family history. Good or bad, it matters." She snagged a spot right next to the star instead of hidden in the back where it belonged.

Cindy eyed the decoration and considered moving it, but something stopped her.

"What exactly is going on with you two, anyway?" MJ asked after a beat, trying to sound casual, and failing completely.

"Honestly? I have no idea what's going on," she confessed, happy to have this conversation with her sister.

They had no secrets, and MJ had always been her sounding board where Jack was concerned. Where everything was concerned, really.

She hung a tiny angel while MJ waited for the rest of the answer.

"We've been spending a lot of time together," she finally said. "Sometimes it feels...nice. Other times, it's awkward. Mostly, it's very familiar and fun." Cindy laughed lightly. "Fun more than anything. After all, it's Jack."

"And he's fun," MJ agreed. "Listen, Cin, don't get in your head about this time together. You two were married for twenty years. You share a child. And you're so natural together. I just watched you with him last night and marveled at how you two are so much alike."

Were they? "Well, we're co-workers right now, technically. But I'd be lying if I said I didn't feel something."

MJ put a hand on her shoulder, the ornaments forgotten as her whole face registered nothing but tenderness.

"You always loved him," she said gently. "And if I'm being honest? I sat there last night and wondered why the heck you and Jack never found a way back to each other."

"Oh, you're just a romantic," Cindy said, but the truth was, she'd been wondering the same thing. "You know what happened. Life got in the way. He loved his job, the travel, the spotlight. I loved the lodge, being rooted here. We tried and we...didn't make it."

And ten years later, it was actually hard to remember why.

"But you never stopped loving each other."

Cindy hung one more festive Santa ornament and then lost the burning need to control the decorating. Now *that* was proof that she really was confused.

"Maybe not," she murmured, dropping onto the sofa with a sigh.

Quiet while she watched her sister humming and hanging, Cindy's mind drifted back to Henry Lassiter. Every time she and MJ had a moment together, Cindy decided it wasn't the right time.

The fact was, she had a solution to their problems long term, but she wasn't sure if MJ would be willing to pay the price. Maybe if she—

Suddenly, the front door creaked open and one of their guests walked into the wide entryway, dusting snow from his navy peacoat.

"Oh, hello, Matt," MJ said quickly, her whole face brightening as she looked over her shoulder at him. "I thought you were having lunch in town today."

Cindy hadn't seen much of Matt Walker, the man who'd come the day after Thanksgiving and showed no sign of checking out of Cabin Five.

He'd kept a low profile, not skiing at all, to her knowledge, but she had noticed him in and out of the kitchen a few times, chatting with MJ.

"I am headed into town," he said. "But I left—"

"Your gloves in the mudroom," MJ finished. "I set them on the counter for you."

"Thank you." He held up his bare hands. "I got very chilly taking my morning walk. But I couldn't turn around because I found the little…I guess you'd call it a river."

"That would be generous," MJ said on a laugh, swiping back a strand of hair. "That's Moose Creek. It's best in the spring when the snow melts and the stream is in full force. Unless it floods. Now it's just icy and a little treacherous, so be careful down there."

"I bet it's beautiful in the spring," he said, looking at MJ like the "it" he was talking about might be…the woman in front of him.

"Everything comes alive," MJ told him, her blue eyes glinting like…like *she* was the one coming alive.

Well, well, *well*.

Cindy sat quietly and watched the exchange, her jaw gaping as she realized Matt hadn't even noticed she was in the room. But he certainly noticed MJ—couldn't tear his gaze away, in fact.

Cindy studied the guest who, up until now, had just been the guy who was paying full price for their most expensive cabin. He had rented a black Escalade, which he took out fairly frequently, but he didn't ski and he didn't…say why he was here all alone.

Matt Walker was probably sixty-six, maybe sixty-seven years old, with a few silver streaks in short chestnut hair. He wore glasses, had a mustache, sported the healthy glow of a tan, and had broad shoulders that looked like he'd been no stranger to hard work during his life.

Matt took a few steps closer, ignoring the tree but

looking directly at MJ. "I'd love to see this place in the spring. Can I book for April?"

"Absolutely!"

Cindy sat up a little bit, the movement enough to pull Matt's attention.

"So nice to see you out of your office, Ms. Kessler," he said.

"Oh, it's just Cindy, please. Yes, I'm the family workaholic. Guilty as charged."

"You have a great lodge," he said. "And you..." He turned back to MJ as if he simply had looked elsewhere for too long. "Run the best kitchen in these mountains. I might have to walk an extra mile, but those scones were worth it."

MJ's cheeks turned even pinker. "I knew you liked them, so there's a small container of a few extras next to your gloves."

"Thank you," he said, eyes twinkling as he turned back to the tree. "You certainly have your work cut out for you. Do you want help with the top?"

"We'll get help when my grandson shows up after school. With the ladder and a lot of direction, he'll get the star up there."

"Ah, Benny," he said. "The resident smarty-pants."

MJ laughed, but Cindy was just a little surprised that this guest had been making friends and getting to know the people at the lodge. She'd hardly talked to him. Admittedly, she'd been a little preoccupied with Jack.

"Well, then, I'll let you get to work," he said,

gesturing toward the tree. "I'll grab those gloves—and scones—and slip out the back. Have fun, ladies."

With that, he disappeared toward the kitchen, with MJ smiling even after he was gone.

"My, my, my," Cindy said, tucking her feet under her on the sofa. "Where have I been this past week?"

MJ reached into a box. "Getting reacquainted with Jack."

She'd walked right into that. "While you're flirting with Matt Walker of Cabin Five."

She shot straight up. "I do not *flirt*, thank you very much."

"No, you just make extra scones and...blush."

"Stop it."

"No," Cindy said on a laugh that only a sister would understand. "He likes you, MJ, and I'm going out on a limb to say it just might go both ways."

MJ shot her a look. "No one likes me, Cin."

"Everyone likes you," Cindy corrected. "How much time have you been spending with that guest?"

"A little, here and there. You don't have to act like I'm *fraternizing* or something."

Cindy snorted. "Whatever that is. And I think it's great."

"Oh, look." MJ dangled an ornament. "Mom always liked these miniature ski poles shaped as a Christmas tree."

"Change the subject much?" Cindy pointed at her, pushing up to rehang a bright red ball because seeing where MJ put it actually hurt. "He's nice, though. Where is he from? What does he do? Does he have a family?"

"He doesn't talk much about that," MJ said. "I think he's from Florida. Mostly we just chat and..."

"Fraternize." Cindy gave a playful elbow jab. "Hey, it's nice to have the heat off Jack and me for a change."

"It's not off," MJ quipped as she reached for her phone and read the screen. "Gracie's on her way with Benny. They'll be here in half an hour." She pressed the small of her back. "Time for a break and some tea."

"Good. I want to talk to you about something anyway."

"Please drop the subject of Matt Walker."

"Maybe," Cindy joked. "But sadly, what I want to talk about is not your favorite subject."

MJ frowned. "That sounds like...money. I thought things were looking up."

"They are," she said. "Let's have tea and I'll tell you."

A few minutes later, they sat alone at the big farm-house table, with MJ's elderberry tea and two of those scones Matt raved about. Late afternoon winter sun poured over them as Cindy told MJ about the man Gracie had met who was interested in investing in Snowberry.

"So, he'd get a piece of the business?" MJ asked, breaking her pastry. "Like a percentage of our profits?"

"Which are so meager it doesn't amount to much," Cindy assured her. "But if we use his money for big ticket items—like all new bathrooms in the lodge and the cabins, work on the roof, and some improvements in this kitchen—we'd still have enough left over to run a really aggressive ad campaign and pay next year's taxes."

"And this year's?" MJ asked.

"I think we're going to cover them," Cindy said, crossing her fingers. "Think about this, too, MJ. After we've done the renovations, we can charge more, we'll get more business, and he'll make his investment back faster. He has to have 'skin in the game,' as he says."

"But that kind of money?" MJ lifted her brows. "That's a lot of skin."

"Which is why a ten percent partnership is really a good deal for us. It's way less than what a bank would charge for interest. And we both know we can't get to where we need to be without some fat cash, and this is it."

MJ sipped her tea, looking out the windows, considering it all. "What do you know about him?"

"Henry? He's very nice, has tons of property investments. And Gracie liked him so much she introduced us."

"My daughter is usually a good judge of character." She made a face. "Except for Sam Sutton. We all make mistakes."

Cindy rolled her eyes at the mention of Benny's father. He'd been a serious boyfriend who grew shockingly *unserious* after he found out Gracie was pregnant. She thought they were going to get married, but he took off for a "job" in Las Vegas and told her the best he could do was send some money now and then.

"But we got Benny," Cindy said, thinking of how that

was all the same year Jack left—such dark days. "And he's a win."

"He is, although I've barely seen him this past week." MJ turned her phone over to see if Gracie had texted. "I can't wait to get him working on that tree."

Cindy broke off a bite of scone. "You'll need to agree to this deal before I go through with it," she said. "We own this place fifty-fifty, and I can't—and won't—go forward if you're not comfortable."

"Oh, Cin, I don't understand business like you do."

"Don't sell yourself short. You know every person who's ever stayed here, what their favorite dessert is, and how fast they ski. Your memory for our guests is down-right freaky."

"Because of my photo albums. Which reminds me..." MJ leaned in with a playful smile. "I need to get Matt Walker's picture and add him to the collection."

Cindy laughed and pointed her scone at her. "I knew you liked him!"

"No, I don't. You know I take a picture of every guest who stays here." She gestured to the row of albums. "Why would he be any different?"

"Because he makes you blush."

MJ looked down at her own pastry, that color rising. "So, what do you want to do about the Henry person?" she asked, obviously changing the subject.

"Make a decision together, I guess," Cindy said. "As I understand it, we'll each get five percent less from our profits. But since the influx of capital would allow us to renovate and potentially double our business, I think it really means much more security for us and for the girls."

MJ lifted a shoulder. "I might be interested. But, goodness, Cindy. No one has ever owned an inch of this place but a Starling."

"I know," Cindy said. "And part of me thinks that's how it should stay. But another part of me—the one with the spreadsheets and sleepless nights? She thinks this might be the answer."

"I need to consider it," MJ said. "And I'd like to meet him."

"You might have met him already," Cindy said. "He said he came over here and scoped the place out, walked the property, went into the ski shed."

"I don't remember that," MJ said. "But we have had a lot of walk-throughs with the sleigh. Can I set up something more official?"

"Of course," Cindy said. "That's the next natural step." A movement outside the window caught her eye—a flash of red as Benny zoomed by.

A second later, the back door burst open. "Let's decorate a tree!" he exclaimed, rushing to MJ. "Did you save the star for me, Grandma?"

She hugged him and kissed his head, straightening his little glasses. "I sure did, Benny. Where's your mommy?"

"In the ski shed. Nicole asked her to work this afternoon."

"Oh, that's right," Cindy said, remembering that Nicole was going to try skiing again, this time with

Brianna. She'd asked Cindy not to mention it to Jack, hoping she could surprise him with good news when she finally got her ski legs back.

"Can I see the tree?" Benny pleaded. "I heard it's huge!"

"It is that." MJ got up, scone, tea, and investments forgotten in the face of her darling grandson. "I'll be right back, Cin."

"Take your time," she said. "I'll finish this scone and send a text to Henry. Benny, don't let her do haphazard decorating."

"I don't know what that means," he said in his boyish voice as they walked off.

"I don't think I've ever heard you say those words." Cindy laughed. "Just look at the tree and you'll know."

She heard their laughter and chatter as they walked back to the great room. Cindy sat for a moment in the quiet, picking up her phone to text Henry. The conversation had gone well, and she was one step closer to getting all she'd ever wanted—security.

Just then, she heard the sound of bells and looked outside.

There, Jack was bringing in a sleigh full of happy riders—wearing his full 1800s regalia, top hat and all, making the event memorable and Instagram-perfect.

Even from here, he looked handsome and dear and familiar and wonderful, and that same old ache filled her whole body.

So maybe security wasn't *all* she wanted in the world.

Part of her—a big, emotional, romantic, lonely part of her—wanted a second chance with Jack Kessler.

Chapter Twelve

Nicole

For reasons that made absolutely zero sense, Nicole found herself once again standing in the shadows of the Snow Park Lodge at the base of Deer Valley, ski boots pinching and stomach churning.

Why did she keep agreeing to this?

She could have just stayed at Snowberry to help Mom and MJ decorate the tree, but she didn't want to bail on Brianna, especially after Gracie had agreed to cover for them at the shed for a couple of hours so they could go afternoon skiing.

Knowing that today would be "the day," Nicole had laid in bed that morning staring at the ceiling and asking herself if she was out of her mind.

And yet here she was...trying again. Terrified, sweating in the chilly weather despite the bright pink jacket she wore, vibrating from head to toe.

"I really think today is going to go better than with your dad." Brianna bounced slightly in her ski boots. Her cheeks were rosy from the wind, but she hadn't even zipped up her jacket—a blinding neon blue—as she took in the action on the snow-covered base of the mountain.

Nicole gave a weak smile, pulling on her face covering. "I appreciate your optimism, Bri. But optimism never got a chicken down the mountain."

"You're not a chicken!"

"Tell that to my stomach—the one that's about to hurl."

Bri laughed, tossing a thick blond ponytail behind her shoulder as she buckled her helmet. "No one is going to hurl."

Nicole wasn't so sure.

"Come on." Brianna held out her gloved hand and pulled Nicole to her feet, jutting her chin toward the rack where the skis waited ominously for their death slide. "We'll take Carpenter up, and I swear we can stick to Success. It's a super mellow green run."

"No bunny hill?" She swallowed a lump of nerves that rose in her throat. "The Snowflake lift looks awfully inviting."

Brianna shot her a look and pulled a pair of goggles over her eyes. "I don't do bunny hills, Nic, and neither should you."

Nicole groaned audibly as they pulled their two sets of skis and poles off the rack and plopped them into the fluffy snow.

Despite the fact that she hadn't skied in nineteen years—not counting one run down the bunny hill with Dad—Nicole knew every run, trail, and lift in Deer Valley. In all the surrounding resorts, too.

And she knew Success was a basic green run. A trainer for kids and beginners. Aside from throwing yourself off a cliff, it was nearly impossible to get legitimately hurt on a gentle slope like that.

But her trauma had teeth. It clawed up her spine every time she stood at the top of a ski run, no matter how mild, no matter how tame.

But this time she had Brianna, a great instructor and trusted friend. Without Dad, it felt like the emotional stakes were lower, and Nicole might actually get out of her fear-addled head and let her body glide and slide. Even fall—just not into a tree well.

Nicole didn't care if she let Brianna down on the slopes. They'd laugh about it. But Dad was a champion skier, and he was her father, the man whose approval and praise Nicole craved deeply.

But with her bestie, there should—theoretically, at least—be far less pressure. She hoped.

Nicole swallowed hard and got into the line for Carpenter Express. Nearby, kids in pastel helmets and instructors in matching jackets darted around her like cartoon characters, fearless and fast.

Nicole tugged at her mittens, hating how rigid her body already felt.

Brianna glanced at her and gave her a gentle nudge with the tip of her pole. "Hey. You got this."

No, actually, she *didn't* have it.

She took a calming breath as they took their lift seats and started the move. No one who skied was immune to the beauty of a ride up the mountain. The Carpenter lift was slow and scenic, and as stunning as any of them.

All around, the sky was a bright winter blue, cloudless and peaceful. The sun lit the crystalline snow so the whole mountain sparkled like sugar. Swinging in a light breeze, they passed over tightly spaced aspens and winding trails peppered with powdery moguls.

Nicole looked down and watched skiers in the distance carving down the side of the mountain in perfect S-curves.

"You good?" Brianna grinned brightly, her excitement to get on the slopes palpable.

"No, but you're a true friend for staying on Success with me." Nicole nudged her. "I'm sure Empire is calling your name."

"Oh, please." She waved a dismissive gloved hand. "Empire will be there all season. I'd rather ski a hundred greens with you all day than rip the crazy double blacks by myself."

Nicole rested her head on Brianna's shoulder, grateful for such a dear friend. "I just want to be able to tell him I did it."

"You will," her friend said, knowing exactly who Nicole meant. "It'll be fun, Nic."

"Yeah? Define fun."

"That." Brianna pointed to the rugged ridges and hundreds of trees.

Nothing about any of that was fun anymore. It had been once—to a little girl who felt fearless and fast. A six-, seven-, eight-year-old who had the most supportive father cheering her on down every run.

Mom had skied back then, too, and they frequently went as a family. But it wasn't Cindy's voice she heard in her head. And it wasn't Cindy who'd been with her the day she nearly died.

They reached the top and skied off the lift. Nicole wobbled slightly but managed to stay upright. The snow was groomed, even after a full morning of December skiing, soft but packed.

The Success trail waited just off to the right, wide and easy.

She could do this, she told herself. Anyone who'd taken one lesson could do this. A girl who'd once imagined that she would be the championship skier her father was? *She* certainly could do this.

"And we're off," Bri called, giving herself a push toward the trail. "Success on Success!"

This run started out like most greens—wide, open, and relatively shallow. Nicole ignored the fact that she was surrounded by kids and beginners and focused on keeping her skis somewhat parallel as she made tiny S's in the snow and used her poles to push forward.

The run took her through some scattered trees, which Nicole tried to ignore, and then shifted into a short, steeper section before leveling out.

She skidded to a stop at the top of the hill, gulping hard.

"You got this, girl!" Bri shouted as she flew past and headed down the hill like a pro, gliding and swerving with a freakish amount of confidence and grace. "Woohoo!"

Nicole remembered when she could ski like that. As a *child!* She remembered the feeling of the edges of her skis slicing beautifully through the snow, the S-curves winding in her wake like something out of a YouTube tutorial.

A person didn't completely lose that skill, did they? Only if fear erased all muscle memory.

Today, fear made her knees feel like Jell-O in lead containers, and she struggled to get a deep breath of cold, crisp air.

"Just do it, Nic," she ground out the words to herself before pushing forward down the slope.

Ten turns into the steep part, her legs locked up. The slope felt more abrupt than it looked from the top. The trees clustered tighter. Her breath quickened.

Bri was ahead, glancing back, encouraging her. "Just edge into the hill a little more, Nic! Let the skis do the work!"

But Nicole couldn't think. She could only feel—her heart thudding, her breath hitching. Her poles trembled in her gloves. Her knees wanted to bend but her thighs screamed. One ski slid faster than the other. They crossed, and her weight shifted the wrong way.

And down she went. Hard.

Right into a snowbank on the side of the run.

Not a terrible fall, but it didn't matter. Both her stupid beginner-level skis had popped off her feet, and her poles were splayed across the run ten feet away.

Humiliation flushed through her in a hot wave.

Brianna skidded to a stop next to her, effortlessly grabbing Nicole's poles on the way. "You okay, Nic?"

Nicole nodded quickly, still sitting in the snow,

breathing hard. "Fine. Totally fine. This is hard. Are you sure it's a green? It seems so steep."

"It's just that one part." She held out a hand. "Here, let me help you up. You're good."

But her throat was tight and her eyes were burning and she was *not good*.

Nicole shook her head. She didn't want help. She didn't want anything except for this very, very bad idea to be over.

She got herself up slowly, brushing off snow. "Let's just get down," she muttered.

It took them twenty minutes to get back to Snow Park Lodge. Nicole skidded down the rest of Success like a terrified beginner, every turn a negotiation. She barely heard Brianna's encouraging words.

By the time they popped off their skis and clomped inside, she was shaking with frustration.

The inside of the lodge was warm and golden, with antler chandeliers hung above cozy wooden tables and Christmas lights everywhere.

A roaring fire crackled in the stone hearth at the far end of the room, flanked by snow-sprayed artificial trees covered in tinsel.

Skiers ended their days sharing stories and snacks and bourbon maple cider.

Nicole let the warmth envelop her as she made her way to a table by the window and dropped into the seat with a grunt of bone-deep frustration.

Brianna peeled off her gloves. "Okay. That was...a good start."

Nicole rested her forehead in her hands. "I can't do this."

"You can. You took a fall. You didn't die. You'll try again."

Nicole sighed. "Maybe I'm just not meant to ski."

Bri leaned in. "Do you *want* to ski again?"

The truth was, she wasn't sure. Part of her wanted to conquer this. She wanted to feel that rush again, the speed, the freedom, the sheer power of beating the mountain.

But there was also a part of her that wanted to be a non-skier who hid in the lodge with a mug of cider and watched everyone else have a blast.

"I don't know," she admitted.

"Rough day out there?"

Nicole lifted her head at the male voice, blinking at a man who stood a few feet away, ski jacket on, goggles around his neck, gorgeous blue eyes trained on her.

"I heard the conditions off the Snowflake lift are brutal," he added with a tease in his voice.

The ski patrol guy! The one who'd helped her up last week when she was here with her dad. "Cameron?" she asked, suddenly remembering his name.

"Yep. So you can't be that rattled by the mountain," he said, taking a step forward and adding a smile that was somewhere between crooked and adorable. "Your memory still works."

He was in uniform—navy ski pants, a red jacket with a white cross on the shoulder. It all only made him even better-looking. "Nicole, right?"

"Right," she said, sitting up straighter. "You seem to show up at my low points in life."

"I better do something about my timing." He grinned at her and glanced at Brianna. "You're an instructor, right? I've seen you giving lessons."

She nodded. "Sometimes. I'm Brianna, and I'm here as best friend, not instructor."

"Nice to meet you, Brianna." He instantly returned his gaze to Nicole, looking concerned. "I thought you were calling it for good last time. I'm glad to see you're not a quitter."

Oh, but she was *such* a quitter. A capital Q Quitter. The quittiest of all the quitters. She never wanted to put those planks on her feet again and she never wanted to lose control or fall in snow or...or...

Wait. *Was* she a quitter? Really?

"Yeah, I'm trying," she said, sounding so weak but at least she didn't disagree.

"That's all you can do," he said. "Otherwise, the mountain wins that battle."

She shrugged. "I fell on Success, which pretty much means the mountain won the whole war."

"That hill halfway down?" He shrugged. "It's not really a green. I mean, it's part of a green, but I've fallen there before."

Probably when he was four, but she smiled at him, appreciating the kind words.

"Nicole's working on getting back into it after a long hiatus," Brianna said, putting a hand on her arm. "She's killing it."

Or it was killing her, but she rooted for a smile. "Thanks for the pep talk, you two. This might be my last attempt, though."

"No!" Bri exclaimed. "We're going back out there in ten minutes."

Oh, no, they were not.

"Listen, I gotta go," Cameron said, glancing outside. "I just popped in for a second and saw you. I like to check on my frequent...fallers."

Nicole laughed. "Guess I'm in that club."

He leaned on the back of the chair across from her, holding her gaze with those insanely blue eyes. "I'd be happy to give you a lesson, if you wanted. No charge. And I promise I know every mellow run at DV. Secret ones that no one else can find."

She ignored the rush of butterflies that fluttered through her. "That's nice, Cameron, but...I'm sure you have much more important things to do."

He cocked his head, looking like he didn't agree with that. "Well, the offer stands. Gotta run." With a nod, he turned and managed to walk gracefully away in his boots, leaving both of them looking a little...dazed.

"Umm. What just happened?" Brianna stared at her. "Did you actually *turn down* that gorgeous hunk of ski patrol?"

Nicole took a breath, a little unable to believe it herself. "He was just being nice."

"Very nice. And very cute, friendly, kind, and obviously available. What is wrong with you, Nicole Kessler?"

Nicole rolled her eyes. "He wants a girl who can ski or—oh, I know." The realization hit. "He wants access to my dad. He practically asked for an autograph when we ran into him here last week."

"Sorry, but no. He's completely into you."

Nicole gave her a look.

Bri grinned, eyeing the slopes outside. "All I'm saying is, if you need more reasons to keep skiing? He might be one."

"I don't need reasons to keep skiing," she said glumly. "I need a reason to not be so afraid of falling in the snow." She closed her eyes, disappointed that her fear of skiing might have cost her a ski date with a totally great guy. "So, I probably should see a shrink after all these years, not a ski instructor."

"That I'm not, but I can get you a drink." Brianna pushed up. "You just sit here and..."

Nicole turned and looked out the window, catching sight of Cameron's ski patrol jacket as he zoomed over to the base.

"And watch the wildlife," she finished.

Chapter Thirteen

Cindy

A few days later, Cindy sat behind her desk, ignoring the snowfall outside. In here, she had her own avalanche to worry about—paperwork that she'd been pretending to tackle all morning. All had been abandoned in favor of the phone she now clutched like a lifeline.

Henry Lassiter's lilting tone continued to make the future look brighter and more secure. Also...confusing.

"So just to make sure I understand," Cindy said, hoping he didn't get frustrated with her questions, "if we go forward with this, the funds would be wired directly to our business account in...trenches? Tranches?" She squinted at her hastily scrawled notes. "Things tied to approved renovations, right?"

"You got it, Cindy," he said, no sign of waning patience. "The first portion, what we call the seed tranche, would be initiated within ten business days of executing the partnership agreement and validating the escrow release form. That's contingent on you fronting the initial percentage—it's just a standard collateral measure."

Cindy frowned slightly, clicking her pen nervously. "You mentioned this before. The fifty thousand that we have to put into the account, right?"

"Yes, but don't get too caught up in that," he assured her. "Think of it like a deposit. Very temporary, and will be refunded in full along with the entire amount of $250,000. Our bank requires you to deposit twenty percent to unlock the full capital commitment, just to mitigate risk for both parties. And listen, Cindy, this isn't just me putting up money. This is a strategic partnership." He paused, taking a deep breath. "I really do believe in Snowberry Lodge."

"You've only seen it once," she said. "MJ would love to meet you and, if I know my sister, feed you. We want you to get the full experience, maybe even stay here for a weekend."

"Oh, no. You'd comp that."

"Of course we would. And put you in our best—well, second best—cabin. Best is currently booked."

"As it should be," he replied. "I will not be responsible for taking away one dollar from your lodge by staying in a room or cabin you can book with paying customers. But I'd love to meet MJ. Let me juggle my schedule." She heard a keyboard click in the background. "I do have to go back East for a week or so to close another deal, but I'll be back in Park City right after that. Although it might be very close to Christmas, and I don't want to intrude."

"Oh, you're welcome to spend the holiday with us... and help me understand this deal a little better." She leaned back in her chair and rubbed her temples. "I'm still unclear on where the funds go first. You said something about a lockbox account?"

"Sure," he replied easily. "I know, this jargon is so boring and confusing. I'll try to make it clear. So, what we'd do is open a dual-controlled escrow lockbox. That's just a fancy way of saying the funds are secured in a neutral account managed by a fiduciary party—usually a regional bank. I'll send you a copy of the mock escrow form. Once your seed contribution is verified, we release the first disbursement into your operating account."

"And we'd have to start renovations right away?"

"Oh, no, no. You can wait until you're ready, but if you can squeeze it in during this calendar year, before January first? You'll get a huge tax break. You should talk to your accountant."

She *was* her accountant. "But no break on what I owe on these property taxes, right?"

"No, this will have no impact on that, except to ease the pain of it," he said. "But everything is fully traceable and audited, of course, and then I'm basically on board as an investor. A shareholder, of sorts."

"I've never done anything like this," Cindy admitted, her voice softening. "I just want to be careful. This lodge...it's our family legacy."

"Which is *exactly* why this works," Henry said warmly. "You're not just another real estate client. You're passionate about Snowberry Lodge. I can tell you, as an investor, we love that. And with your experience? You're the ideal partner. We're just giving you the boost to take it into the next iteration—a beautifully remodeled lodge that easily competes with the big hotels."

Her pulse slowed. He made her feel like this wasn't some reckless gamble but a smart, calculated move. Like she was taking control. Saving the lodge, rather than watching it slip through her fingers.

Cindy bit her lip and underlined the word "tranches" in her notebook.

"While I'm out of town," he said, "I'll have my assistant send you everything we discussed—PDFs of the framework, sample agreements, term sheets. It's a lot of legalese, but don't worry. I'll walk you through it. We can do a video call if you like, or you can take it to your attorney first."

"Okay," she said, almost whispering. "Thank you, Henry. Really."

"My pleasure. And Cindy? For what it's worth— you're doing a brave thing. Most people would've sold the place and walked away. I love that you're a fighter. It's a big part of why I want to be on board with Snowberry. I believe in the lodge, and I believe in you."

She smiled faintly. "Yeah. Well. I'm stubborn."

"I like that in a business partner."

They ended the call, and for a moment, Cindy just sat there. Her heart thudded—not with dread, but hope. A real investor. A real plan. Maybe this *could* work. Maybe this was the next chapter in the long story of Snowberry Lodge.

Cindy leaned back in her chair and looked at the twinkling lights outside the office window as night threatened to fall and fall fast. Snowberry looked like a snow globe this time of year—glittering pine trees, smoking chimneys, wreaths on every cabin door. It was magic. And for the first time in months, she could almost see a way forward.

A knock on the office door jolted her out of her thoughts.

Turning, her heart did an unexpected leap at the sight of Jack bracing his arms on the doorjamb. He'd changed from his carriage uniform to a forest green flannel under a shearling-lined coat, snow dusted across his shoulders. His face, ruddy from the cold, broke into a sweet, familiar grin.

"Woman, you work too hard."

She lowered the laptop screen and flipped her notebook over, not really wanting to talk to Jack about the Henry Lassiter plan. She wasn't sure why, but she didn't.

"I'm done for the day," she announced.

"Awesome!" He stepped inside and held her gaze. "My last sleigh ride canceled, and I don't have another until long after dinner. I gave Red some well-deserved time off and I would like you, my dear, to come with me on a sleigh ride."

Her whole body fluttered at the invitation, and the term of endearment. She tried to cover it up by sliding into her safe and secure business mode.

"They canceled?" she asked.

"Rescheduled for tomorrow," he promised her. "Conditions at DV were excellent today and they're wiped out from a day on the slopes. Everyone is saying it's a great ski week."

Everyone but Nicole—another thing she didn't want to mention to him. But only because her daughter asked her not to.

"I appreciate you working so hard, Jack. I'm sure all this powder is making you antsy to get on skis."

He just shook his head, his dark gaze pinned on her as he drew closer. "I don't feel like skiing, Cin. Now, come with me. Copper is all harnessed and ready. You can't keep avoiding taking a sleigh ride with me."

But she could try. Yes, she'd spent plenty of time with him over the last ten days or so. They'd shared meals, talked by the fire late into the night, even perused some old family photo albums, laughing over Nicole's antics as a baby.

But she had yet to find the nerve to get back on that sleigh again, because last time? She darn near kissed him.

"Just making room for paying customers," she added, echoing Henry's excuse.

"Well, this ride is on me." He reached his hand over the desk and, without really thinking about it, she slipped her fingers into his chilly, strong ones. "Please?"

She exhaled, feeling any fight slipping away. "I'd love to."

The snow had stopped by the time Cindy put on a jacket, boots, gloves, and a festive red beanie that Nic had given her last year for Christmas. She walked outside to join Jack, who was cooing in Copper's ear and no doubt slipping him treats to bribe him for another ride.

As he stepped away and turned to her, Cindy's breath caught, slammed with déjà vu at the sight of her ex-husband standing in front of the Snowberry Sleigh.

Behind him, the dark cherrywood and black leather seats gleamed in the lamplight of the antique brass lanterns hanging on the sleigh. It was like time faded away. Instead of Copper, there was another horse, and a younger man who tempted her every time he was nearby.

And he was tempting her again.

"Cute hat," he said, coming closer to give the pom-pom a playful tap. "Still the pretty blonde in a red cap just like the first time we did this."

Had she'd worn a red hat that day? She didn't remember but was touched that he did. "Well, there are silver threads in this blond head. More every day."

He laughed and brushed his own rather salty hair. "No kidding." Then he reached for her hand. "Let me help you up."

He eased her into the sleigh seat, his gloved hand lingering in hers just a beat longer than necessary. As he followed and settled beside her, she let out a silent exhale, but the soft puff of cold air gave away her nerves.

"You think we're going to have a problem?" he asked, giving her a side-eye. "Copper knows this route like he was born for it now, and we don't go anywhere near the places that spook him."

She looked up at him, lost for a moment. Utterly and completely *lost*.

"It's not Copper I'm worried about." Not by a long shot.

He leaned a millimeter closer, his mouth lifting in a sly smile. "I'll behave."

Her heart tumbled as he picked up the reins and clicked at Copper, sharp and sure, proving the horse really had been tamed by the sleigh rides.

Copper set off, clip-clopping over the snowy path that would take them past the cabins and deeper into the property trails.

As they glided along, Jack reached into the back for a red plaid blanket, draping it over their legs. Once they were tucked in, he lifted a shoulder as he adjusted the reins and kept Copper to an uncharacteristically slow pace.

"I'm not used to this speed from Flying Jack," she joked.

"I read the mood of my passengers," he said. "You look like a lady who likes to take her time."

"At certain things," she said, leaning back as she felt tension in her shoulders and neck melt away. "And, wow, this is a good way to end a busy day."

He threw her a smile. "I'm glad you're with me."

"Me, too." Cindy admitted, sneaking a long peek at his profile, another thing she always loved about Jack.

The thought jolted her—*always loved?* Did she still? Of course, they'd been married for twenty years, raised a beautiful daughter together, and had history.

Was that love?

Right now, in this dark, snowy, magical moment? It felt like it could be.

As if he read her mind, he slipped his hand over hers, their gloves pressing together between them.

"That okay?" he whispered as Copper took the next bend a little faster at the last cabin, making her wonder if he meant the handholding or the turning.

"Yes." She squeezed his hand. "It's okay."

"Not terrified?" he teased.

Only of the fact that she couldn't remember a single reason why she'd ever filed those divorce papers. Not one.

The runners shushed through the snow as Copper kept up an easy trot. They followed the wide, rolling trail that climbed gently toward the higher hills. The pine trees stood tall and frosted, all accompanied by the jingle of sleigh bells, and the steady rhythm of Copper's hooves.

"This never gets old," Jack said quietly.

Cindy turned her face toward the chilly wind, but the sleigh's blanket and Jack's warmth beside her kept the cold at bay. "No. It doesn't."

They passed the entrance to the creek, the lantern light catching a glimpse of something between the tree line, near the icy water.

"What's that?"

"Oh, Benny and Red built a fort for...some Christmas surprise they're working on."

"A Christmas surprise? What is it?"

Laughing, he put his arm around her. "If I told you, it wouldn't be much of a surprise, would it?"

She shrugged, deciding he was right. She leaned into Jack, looking out toward the resort. The lift lights glittered, closed for the night but swaying like stars hanging over the mountain.

"It's beautiful out here," she said.

Jack glanced sideways. "Speaking of beautiful...so are you."

She wanted to look away but couldn't. In fact, she wanted to breathe and couldn't do that either.

"Jack," she whispered. "Did you bring me out here to flirt?"

"Just like the first time," he said with a laugh. "In fact..." He gave the reins a tug to the left as they reached the turn to Bluebell Crossing. "I'm in the mood to recreate that night."

If he remembered her hat, then he certainly remembered...their first kiss. The thought of recreating that simply melted her.

"Now, that could be dangerous," she said quietly, but made no effort to move away.

"Copper knows the way," he told her. "I added it to the sleigh ride trail for the longer rides. And every time I'm up there, I think about you."

She sighed.

"I do a lot of that lately," he confessed as Copper trotted up the hill.

"Well, technically, you work for me," she said, fighting the urge to sink into what he was offering—a connection, a romance, a reliving of such happier days.

"I'm not thinking about work," he said. "I'm just... sleigh-riding down memory lane."

She smiled at that, letting silence stretch between

them like a snow-laden branch, delicate and heavy, as his sweet words fell like a few flakes fluttering around them.

"What are you remembering the most?" she finally asked.

"Everything. All the moments and memories. All the love and laughter. I know, I know. I sound like a sappy Christmas card, but it's how I feel being here. And with you. And Nic. The whole family, but mostly you." His words tumbled out, his voice thick with emotion that squeezed her heart.

"Why did you come back, Jack?"

"What do you mean?" He blinked in surprise at the question.

"When Nic asked you to come back here, to do this..." Cindy took a deep breath. "Did you really agree just because you wanted to teach her to ski again? Or you cared about the lodge? Or..."

He inhaled slowly. "Because I missed everything. The lodge. The smell of the air here. This place...it's part of me. I was raised in these mountains, and I lived here for fifty years." He looked at her, eyes full of something soft and sincere. "Truth?"

Her breath caught. "Please," she whispered.

"I didn't come back just for sleigh rides," he said. "I mean, that's what I told myself. But the thought of seeing you...of spending these weeks with you..." He glanced away, laughing easily as he shook his head. "I jumped at the chance, to be honest."

She looked down at the blanket on her lap, her heart thumping against her ribs.

"I was excited when you came back," she said.

"You didn't look excited," he scoffed. "You looked dumbfounded."

She laughed. "Well, I didn't want to admit it, but...I was happy."

"I was happy, too. I'm still happy. Happier than I've been in a long time."

They didn't speak again until the sleigh crested the final hill. There they reached the overlook where two trails connected at a pasture that, in spring, was filled with tiny blue flowers, giving it the name of Bluebell Crossing.

To Cindy, it was, and always would be, where she and Jack had their first kiss.

Even in the waning light, the view was as breathtaking as she remembered—rolling white hills, shadows curling between evergreens, the sky glowing gold and lavender with the last whisper of light, the mountain looming high and holy.

Jack pulled Copper to a stop. "Want to give him a break and walk in the snow?"

"Sure."

They climbed out of the sleigh, hitting the drifts of snow. Cindy turned in a slow circle, taking it all in. The beauty. The stillness. The memories.

"When you look back on our marriage," he said, keeping his arm firmly around her shoulders so her revolution ended facing him. "What do you remember most? What is the memory that flashes into your mind?"

She considered the question for a long time, appreciating it, and wanting to give it an honest answer.

"There are snapshots," she finally said, sliding an arm around him so they could walk around the crossing. "Not like the photo album, but more real life. The moment you said 'I do,' and the look on your face when they put Nic in your arms."

He smiled, squeezing his eyes as though that got him.

"I remember you coming in from working on the property, looking a lot like"—she eased back and brushed his jacket—"this. Rugged and outdoorsy and strong and..." She didn't finish but laughed.

"Say it," he teased.

"Sexy."

He chuckled, liking that. "What else?" he asked, obviously enjoying the answers.

"I remember I used to wake up in the middle of the night." She slowed her step and came to a stop, knowing she was about to confess something she'd never told him, but wanted him to know. "Next to you, of course. You sleep on your back, and I could see your profile in the darkness of our bedroom, your chest rising and falling. I could hear your breath and feel your warmth, our toes touching under the blanket."

She saw him swallow as he looked down at her, silent, listening, remembering.

"That's when I loved you most," she whispered. "Those moments in the middle of the night. I felt so safe and secure, so protected and loved. I was often overwhelmed by how much I loved you. I would kiss your

shoulder. I'd just lean over and press my lips right here..."
She touched the front of his shoulder. "And I would
mouth the words, 'I love you,' over and over."

He let out a soft whimper and closed his eyes. "I slept
through that kind of love?"

"It was my secret."

Without answering, he slid both arms around her,
pulling her into his chest, looking down at her. "When I
think about us, all my senses get involved."

She frowned, searching his face, not following.

"I hear you laughing with MJ in the kitchen, and that
was like music to me. I can smell the baby shampoo on
your hands after you'd bathed Nic and came to cuddle on
the couch with me. I see you rushing to the door to greet
me after a trip..." He flinched. "There were way too many
trips, Cin."

She felt her shoulders sink. "And now you've hit the
bad stuff."

For a long, long time, he looked at her. His gaze was
soft, but not the look of a man about to kiss her. This was
something else entirely.

"I know you've forgiven me," he said. "We've talked
about that, and I know it. But I want to tell you something you need to believe."

She inched back, the sheer force of his words hitting
her. "Yes?"

"I never really stopped loving you, Cindy." His voice
was gruff, and low, and so genuine. "I loved you pretty
much from the day we were here and kissed thirty-plus
years ago, to right this minute and all the ones in

between. I've never loved anyone else, and I don't think I will."

"Oh, Jack." She heard her voice crack. "That's..." *Dizzying*, she thought as she darn near swayed in his arms. "Wow."

He tightened his grip. "I know it's been ten years. I know we hurt each other. But I also know that marrying you was the best thing I ever did and losing you was the worst."

Her eyes stung.

"I'm not asking for a miracle," Jack continued. "But is there any possibility, any at all in heaven or hell, that we could try again?"

She felt the whole world tilt sideways as her next breath caught in her chest. "Are you serious?" she asked on a ragged whisper.

"Yes," he said simply. "I am."

She inched back, pressing her hands to her chest, staring up at him. "Jack..." Of course she wanted to say yes. She wanted to melt into this moment, under the spell of the mountain and the man she'd first kissed in this spot.

It would be so easy. So exciting. Like having a past and a future again, instead of feeling stuck in a slightly dreary present. Like living in color, hearing music, or tasting cake, or...giving in to temptation for something that could hurt her again.

She dug for common sense and a different memory— the ease with which he'd walked away, the look of resignation when she told him it was over, the dozens and dozens of times he chose skiing and work and travel and *something else* over her.

She had no way to believe that could change. What if this was just the memories talking? The magic of the season and the snow? The hope they could recapture something that was so brutally lost?

"Bad idea?" He tried to laugh after her silence lasted a beat too long, clearly taking it as a rejection.

Was it?

"I just..." Biting her lip, she leaned into him, then dropped her head onto his shoulder, his jacket pressing against her cheeks. Vaguely aware that tears slipped through her nearly frozen eyelashes, she clung to him while every emotion a woman could feel ricocheted through her body.

Finally, she lifted her face, looking at him, silent and stunned and...shockingly close to saying yes.

"*Now* I'm dumbfounded," she breathed into a laugh. "And I don't know what to say."

"It's fine. I understand. My time has come and gone and I just...I had to let you know I've been thinking about it. Fantasizing, in fact."

She opened her mouth to say she had, too, but something stopped her. Something protected her. She never wanted to hurt like she had that Christmas Day when he'd taken off to cover a competition and the last thing she'd said was...leave and this marriage is over.

And he left.

For that reason, she couldn't say yes now.

He stepped back and gave a sad smile, tipping his head toward the horse.

"We better get back," he said. "Copper should rest before his last ride."

And Cindy, she realized with a sad thud, was not getting a second first kiss.

Her eyes burned, but she lifted her face and let the snowflakes melt on her cheeks. That way, he'd never know she'd cried.

Chapter Fourteen
Nicole

"Do we have to go to Sugarfall?" Benny asked as Nicole turned onto the side street near her cousin's bakery.

It was ten days before Christmas, and Park City was jammed with tourists, but Nicole found a parking spot and snagged it. "Your mom had to work late on a wedding cake, Benny, and I promised I'd bring you to see her after your choral practice was over."

"But can't we just go home to Snowberry? Santa—er, I mean Grandpa—is waiting for me."

She looked in the rearview mirror, meeting his bespectacled gaze from his safe seat in the back and wishing he were up here next to her. He'd be allowed to ride in the front next year, Gracie said, but she was a very protective single mom, and Nicole respected that.

"You always want me to bring you here when she works late and I pick you up from school," she reminded him. "I believe it has something to do with...cookies."

"We had cookies at practice," he said. "Bad boxed ones that tasted like cardboard covered in Elmer's glue."

She snorted. "You sound more like your great-grandfather every day."

"Well, it's true. They were just bribing us to sing louder."

"Did you?"

He lowered his glasses and gave her a "get real" look, making her laugh. "I just really want to go home and, um, be with Grandpa. We had plans, especially if no one is booked on the sleigh."

"It's booked," she told him as she unlatched her seatbelt. "I looked at the schedule because I had some customers ask and there are not many openings."

"It's booked? Is the whole lodge full yet? The way Aunt Cindy wanted?"

She climbed out and opened his door, beaming at him. "I love that you care so much about the adult stuff, Benny."

"Oh, I do care," he said. "Are we booked? Did she make December?"

Nicole shook her head, ever amused by this child-man, who refused her hand to help him onto the snowy curb. "Benny, you are ten going on forty, you know that?"

"I just...care about that."

"Come on, big guy. Good cookies await. Hand made by your mama. What song do you not sing in the Christmas chorus?"

He moved his mouth, no sound coming out.

"What was that?" she asked.

"*My* version of 'Winter Wonderland.'" He looked up and gave her a very serious look, adjusting his glasses. "Tech moguls don't sing."

She cracked up. "Hey, the only moguls around here are up in the mountains."

"You'll see," he said as they walked toward the shiny gold sign that read *Sugarfall* etched into the wood over the door. When they got there, Nicole pushed open the bakery door, the bell giving a sweet jingle before falling quiet again.

Late afternoon light streamed through the front windows, spilling across empty display cases and chairs already turned upside down on tables. The rush was over, and the tourists had moved from cinnamon rolls and hot chocolate to cocktails and fine dining.

But Sugarfall's scents lingered—warm butter, melted chocolate, and a faint ribbon of coffee that clung to every corner.

"Smells like heaven," Nicole called, peeling off her gloves and tucking them into her coat pocket.

Gracie stepped out from the kitchen doorway, tendrils of her strawberry blond hair falling over her face, a bit of flour streaked across the apron she wore. She was MJ's clone for sure, with lighter red hair and a more intro-verted personality.

"You always say that." Gracie laughed, waving them inside. "There's my Benny boy!" She held out her hands —one with a spatula—for Benny to run to her. But he just shuffled forward.

She cocked her head in fake exasperation. "Hello? Mom-love, please." She shook her hands. "Been waiting all day."

He gave a quick smile. "Can we go back to Snow-berry soon?"

Gracie straightened and looked surprised. "I thought you'd stay while I finish this cake. It's for a Christmas wedding. Want to see?"

He shrugged and let her hug him, then headed past her into the kitchen.

"Did he have a bad chorus practice or something?" Gracie whispered.

"He wants to get home to Red."

Gracie made a face, then slipped an arm around Nicole. "Thanks for picking him up. There's a red velvet cupcake with your name on it. Well, it says 'St. Nick' and has a red Santa cap, but it's still your name."

Hugging her back, Nicole let her cousin lead her deeper into the Sugarfall kitchen, a magically sweet place where the worktables gleamed under bright lights. Stainless-steel bowls and measuring spoons were stacked neatly to the side, but one table was completely taken over by a towering white cake. Buttercream already smoothed its sides to perfection, and some evergreen sprigs lined the bottom layer.

"Everyone's gone for the day," Gracie said, picking up a piping bag. "Have tea, cocoa, whatever you want. I just have to make the roses and add a few last-minute touches to this cake."

"It's gorgeous," Nicole told her. "Where's the wedding?"

Gracie looked over the cake. "Grand Hyatt, of course."

Nicole rolled her eyes and wandered around her cousin's workplace, which was so different from her own.

Benny perched on a chef's stool in front of a tray of white frosted sugar cookies and a fresh glass of milk his mother had prepared. Next to it, a small plate with a Christmas cupcake decorated as Santa's face that did, indeed, say "St. Nick" in fondant letters.

Nicole ruffled his hair as she passed. "Told you it was better than school."

"Did you have cookies at school?" Gracie asked as she coaxed some icing out of the bag with the same tenderness she used to get conversation out of her son.

"Bad ones. Did Grandpa call?"

"No. Were you expecting him to?"

"Not really." He pushed the cookies away. "Can I play a game on your computer in the office?"

Gracie looked up from the cake, searching her son's face. "Sure. You okay, Ben?"

"Yeah, I'm good. I just wanted to, um, do something with Grandpa today."

"Do what?" she asked.

"You know, our secret Christmas present." He grinned. "You're not the only one who has surprises planned this month."

With that, he scurried toward the back, but only made it two steps before he stopped, turned, grabbed a cookie, and rushed off.

Gracie watched him, then closed her eyes. "That boy."

"Not a boy." Nicole took the stool he vacated. "He's a tech mogul. I was just informed."

Gracie smiled, but kept her attention on the icing, quiet as she turned an intricate leaf.

"Gah, you make that look easy," Nicole said.

"It's not easy," Gracie said without looking up. "It's just that after a thousand or so cakes, you stop worrying about ruining them."

"I ruin cookies just by burning the bottoms." Nicole pushed off to get a cup of tea. "So you're still a wizard in my book."

They were quiet while she went through the motions of brewing the tea, the only sound the hum of the kitchen dishwasher and the occasional ding from the office computer where Benny had started playing a game.

When Nicole came back, Gracie's expression had shifted. She was still piping roses, but her eyes were softer and more thoughtful. Every few seconds, she glanced toward the back where Benny had disappeared.

"Everything okay?" Nicole asked.

"I guess," she said on a sigh.

"Benny?"

She nodded. "He's been kind of distant with me. Have you noticed?"

"Well, it's Christmastime and he's a kid," Nicole said. "And I've noticed that he's never far from Red, but that's always been the case."

"Right? Do you think that's healthy?"

"Yes! Red's his great-grandfather and Benny's always been an old soul. Doesn't shock me that he wants to hang around with an eighty-two-year-old who is the closest thing to a real live Santa who ever lived."

"But he just..." She exhaled like whatever she was about to say pained her. "He really doesn't have any friends, Nic. Did you see him talking to the other kids at school when you picked him up after chorus?"

Nicole thought about the groups of nine- and ten-year-olds waiting for their rides and, she was right—Benny had been separate from all of them.

"I don't think he loves chorus," she said, trying to be vague instead of selling out her beloved little Benny. "Maybe those aren't his people. I mean, there wasn't a tech mogul in the bunch."

Gracie smiled at that. "I forced him to be in chorus so he'd make friends, but it didn't work."

"He'll be fine," Nicole assured her. "He'll make more friends when he gets older. And in the meantime, he has us and Red."

Gracie fussed with a rose petal, smoothing the icing with a tiny tool. "It's why I have been holding off on the dog."

"I thought you were worried about the commitment and caretaking."

"That's just what I say," she admitted, speaking softly enough that Benny, a notorious eavesdropper, couldn't hear. "I'm afraid if he has a dog, he won't make any effort to have friends. It'll just be Benny and his dog, and that would be enough for him. He has no siblings, no friends, no cousin like you and I had. And Red is getting older and..." She couldn't even finish the sentence.

"Don't worry about things that haven't happened yet, Gracie." But she knew that was wasted advice on Gracie, who didn't have her mother's blind optimism. Aunt MJ saw the glass as half full—Gracie was pretty sure someone was going to knock it over and get cut by a shard.

"I know what it's like to be a shy kid," she said. "It makes life harder."

"Benny's not shy," Nicole said. "He's just twenty steps ahead of the average ten-year-old and doesn't have the patience to wait for their brains to catch up."

"And he doesn't have a father," Gracie continued, clearly ready to let out some things that had been working on her heart. "There are no men around the lodge, he has no male figure in his life except for Red."

Nicole rubbed her arms, thinking about some of the cryptic—and weirdly hopeful—things her mom had said when they had coffee in the ski shed this morning.

"You never know..." she said in a slightly sing-song voice. "There might be a man around here."

Gracie looked up, fast enough to almost mess up. "What? Who? What don't I know? Did you meet someone?"

Nicole laughed and reached over to start on her red velvet Santa. "No—well, actually, maybe I did, but that's not what I mean. My parents are..." She lifted her eyebrows and wiggled them.

Gracie abandoned the cake and stood straight. "So, we're not imagining it, are we?"

"We?"

"My mom and I have been talking about how great they are together. Mom is obsessed with how they are the couple that should never have broken up. I thought maybe it was her typical wishful thinking."

"I know Aunt MJ loves my dad," Nicole said. "I don't think this is her wishful thinking. I'm pretty wishful about it, too."

Gracie reached for a tray of evergreen sprigs, ready to attack the cake's second layer. "What does Aunt Cindy say about it?"

"Not a lot, but I know she's terrified of getting hurt again. I mean, she hasn't told me point blank that she's still in love with him, but I know her well. She protects herself." Nicole took a bite of icing and cake, and moaned, closing her eyes. "Are you kidding me?" she asked around a mouthful.

Gracie smiled. "I never kid about cupcakes, Nic. But your mom. Do you think she's going to get hurt again? I love having Uncle Jack around, but I do not want her to go through losing him a second time. It was all the same year that Sam ditched my pregnant self and..." She shook her head. "I say it's better to be safe than have your heart destroyed."

"I don't know," Nicole said.

As she tried to take her time with the cupcake, Nicole studied her cousin, who, at thirty-five, was beautiful, accomplished, kind...and protected her heart the way she protected Benny from the world. But then, she'd been hurt by Sam Sutton, and spent the last ten years building a business and raising a son.

Gracie looked up from a sprig she was placing on the second layer. "I will say this. Everything at Snowberry just feels better when Uncle Jack's there."

Nicole smiled, nodding in agreement. "He does bring the spirit, but it's Christmas, so..."

"He makes things lighter," Gracie said. "And ever since he got there, it's been good. The sleigh rides are running, guests are happier, and your mom doesn't seem quite so focused on the business. I can't remember the last time we had so many dinners in that big kitchen, the whole table just full of family. He's like a human magnet, your dad."

"He's special," Nicole agreed, affection welling up. "Look, I'd be lying if I said I didn't love the idea of a second chance for those two. They're my parents. In my mind, they belong in the same house, in the same room, together. And they do still love each other. A blind man can see that. But I guess sometimes love isn't enough."

Gracie finished a sprig and reached for another. "What's this about a new guy you mentioned?"

"I did?"

"Slipped it right in there and said 'maybe I did' when I asked if you'd met someone." She pointed the evergreen at her. "Did you think I was going to let that slide by?"

"Of course not. He's...just a ski patrol dude I bumped into both times I made the massive and horrible mistake of trying to get down Deer Valley's itty-bitty green run and failed."

Gracie sighed, angling her head to look at Nicole. "I know it's hard for you, Nic. It's understandable."

"Is it? Because I don't understand it," Nicole admitted. "I get out there with all the desire and motivation and determination and ability that a daughter of Flying Jack Kessler would have on skis and, wham! Frozen. In fear, not in snow."

Gracie took a few steps closer, nothing but love and sympathy in her blue eyes. "Girl, you have every right to be frozen in fear."

"Nineteen years later?"

Gracie just looked at her. "I was there, Nic. I was on that mountain when Uncle Jack saved your life. I didn't see you fall, I didn't see him dig you out of that tree well, and I wasn't down there suffocating with you. But I saw you come down at the end and, honey, you have every right to be afraid to ski again."

"Thank you for saying that." Nicole reached for her. "I'm so tired of feeling like a failure because I'm scared."

Gracie took her hand and squeezed. "It's understandable, but you can conquer that fear."

"What if I don't want to?" Nicole closed her eyes and took a deep breath. "Never mind. Forget that. Of course I want to. I miss skiing like other people miss breathing. I love it up there. I love the feeling of sailing down a slope, in control, in nature, bold and fast and thrilled by every turn. I miss the views, the sky, the feeling of being connected to that mountain. It hurts *not* to ski and it hurts to try."

Gracie gave a soft grunt. "You *were* born to ski. I never loved it like you did, and Benny could take it or leave it. But you? Yeah."

Nicole twisted the edge of the napkin Gracie had thoughtfully put next to the cupcake.

"Twice now I've gone out there, thinking I could just pick it up again. And both times? I could not do it. Do you think I need, like, professional help? I've always rejected the idea of therapy for that accident."

"Maybe the professional help you need is"—she leaned over the counter and gave a hard look—"a cute ski patrol dude."

Nicole laughed. "I knew you'd get back to him. I just feel like I should be past this by now."

Gracie came around the counter and put her arms around Nicole. "Sweet cousin of mine, please don't be so hard on yourself." She drew back and searched Nic's face, no doubt rooting for wisdom and the right words. "You went through something terrifying. PTSD doesn't just fade because you think it should. It took *me* a long time to get over it, and I was just waiting at the base for you guys to come down. Then I saw the helicopters and lights and all the patrols..." Her eyes shuttered with the memory. "It was a terrible day, and I honestly thought I'd lost you."

Nicole's chest tightened as she hugged Gracie.

"I keep trying to do it for other people," Nicole said. "Dad. Bri. Maybe this guy. But it doesn't stick. I need something more."

Gracie's eyes grew fierce with conviction. "Then that's your answer. You need to conquer the fear for your own reason. For *you*. You have to want to push those poles and trust those skis and ignore the trees and the people and everything else but flying down that slope."

Nicole smiled. "You always know what to say, Gracie."

"Of course I do. I'm your cousin."

Before Nicole could reply, Benny came back in, nothing but impatience on his little features. "Is the cake done? Grandpa is waiting for me."

"Grandpa is probably asleep in his recliner," Gracie said, picking up her tools and carrying them to the sink. "Ten more minutes and we can go home."

"But it'll be too late," he whined, grabbing a cookie and picking up his milk.

"Too late for what?" she asked.

He filled his mouth with a cookie and shrugged, feigning innocence as he slipped back into the office without answering.

"See?" Gracie said. "I feel like he's hiding something."

"He is," Nicole agreed. "But I'm telling you, it's Christmas. He's probably painting you a picture or some-thing and Red's helping him."

"Benny? Painting?"

"Okay. Coding."

"Wait'll you have a kid." She added a sly smile. "Speaking of, tell me more about the ski patrol guy. You know, the one who's going to be the reason you need and want to ski again."

She choked softly. "Speaking of wishful thinking."

"You got to have a little of that if you're ever going to ski again, Nic."

Nicole just nodded, knowing she was right. "All I know is his name is Cameron and…" She got up and brushed the crumbs from her hands. "I'll help you clean up."

"And what?" Gracie pressed.

Nicole smiled. "He's really cute. That's it."

"Well, that's a start."

Chapter Fifteen
Red

"One more, Grandpa. One more that goes viral!" Benny sat hunched over in the front seat of the sleigh they'd just taken from Jack so he could warm up before his next customers arrived, who weren't due for well over an hour. "If we can do that, Aunt Cindy will book the rest of the month, and then I promise we'll come clean."

"We better," Red muttered. "I don't like lyin', Benny-bean. I don't like it all."

Benny nodded, a little guilt darkening his golden-brown eyes behind snow-dampened glasses.

As they made their way up the trail, the runners of the sleigh cut a clean hiss over the fresh-packed snow, a sound Red had come to love even when he pretended otherwise. The trail that curved toward Moose Creek shimmered with frost, every pine branch weighed heavy with powder from last night's storm.

Clouds hung low, turning the afternoon light bluish gray. Red's breath puffed in small clouds over his nearly frozen beard. Beside him, Benny sat with his gloved hands hugging the phone like it was made of gold.

Red adjusted his Santa hat. The thing had slid sideways on the ride out and now poked one eyebrow like it was conspiring against him.

"You know this is lunacy," he muttered. "A man my age, freezing parts of myself better left unfrozen, all for the sake of a blasted phone screen."

Benny's grin didn't budge. "One more video, Grandpa. That's all we need. It'll be epic."

"Epic? I don't trust that word." Red curled his lip and tugged the reins lightly to guide Copper off the main lodge trail and onto the narrow spur that led to Moose Creek. "Epic usually means I'm going to make a fool of myself."

"Grumpy Santa is so popular!" Benny said, as if that covered any foolishness. "I heard Aunt Cindy ask Grandma MJ if she knew what some people were talking about when they checked in and asked to meet him!"

"All the more reason to come clean with our lie, little man."

"We will, we will," Benny said. "But this video is going to be—"

"I know. Epic."

"Even better than the hot cocoa review when you pretended to burn your tongue and spit out marshmallows!" He slapped his leg with a giggle. "We got like five hundred new followers and a hashtag—spittingsanta! It was better than the *Jingle Bells* rant."

Red chuckled. "Well, that dumb kids' song—'Jingle bells, Santa smells'—had to be put away. I don't care if it's just third-grade humor. It offends."

The whole bit had been good, though. Benny had

laughed so hard he nearly dropped the phone. Plus, it got what the kid wanted most—thousands of likes and views and...whatever else he considered internet currency.

"Remind me again," Red said, "what's so perfect about freezing our tails off at a snow fort when we could be in the lodge eatin' pie?"

Benny bounced in his seat. "Because people loved the fort! I've seen comments asking about it—like, is it real, can you book it, can Grumpy Santa give a tour? We'll show it off. You'll look all cranky about it, and then boom—viral."

Red snorted, though part of him—some small, treacherous part—was proud of how sharp the boy's instincts were. Marketing was half smoke and mirrors anyway. Benny understood that better than most grown men.

Copper's ears flicked back, probably because he sensed the change in terrain as they neared the creek. The last time they'd come up here, it had been warmer and morning—he and Benny had walked to make their snow fort and video. But it was easier now with Copper dragging them along.

As they neared the creek, all was still, with the water frozen and the meadow beyond it untouched except for some distant deer tracks. Through the trees, Red spotted the fort—a crooked little wall of snow blocks, lopsided but charming.

Jack told him Cindy had seen the little snow structure, and he'd brushed off questions about it as a "Christmas surprise."

Red would be much happier when this subterfuge was over. It didn't sit well with him to lie to his family. Yeah, yeah, Gracie would be all bent out of shape. But like Benny said, if they saved December and got that tax money? His mama would get over a little rule-breaking.

"All right," Red said, tightening his grip on Copper's reins, the horse prancing a bit before the fort came into clear view. "Lay it on me. What's the grand scheme?"

As soon as Red slowed the horse to a stop, Benny hopped down, snow squeaking under his boots. He scampered around to Copper's head, reaching up to pat his nose.

"Here's the plan," he said, as mature as a grown man running a business meeting. "You sit there looking all grouchy like you hate the fort, but this is where your elves live...something like that. You always make up the funniest stuff."

"'Cause I'm a comedic genius."

Benny ignored the aside. "Off-camera, I'm going to blast you with a snowball. And I mean blast. Right in the face."

Red cocked his head. "You don't have to sound *that* delighted about it."

Benny giggled. "You're gonna get so mad! You'll be grumbling about elves with attitude. You know. You look across the creek and pretend to see them. Runaway elves! Little rebels! Bad creatures! All your funny stuff. Then you give Copper a snap of the reins and go running off after them, alongside the creek, with you waving your hat and having a whole grumpy moment. And then I'll hit you again with a big bomber!"

He practically danced with joy and Copper whinnied, cold and not enjoying the stop at all.

Red raised his brows. "You like that part a little too much, kid."

"It'll be fun."

"Not for me."

"It'll make you grumpier!" Benny insisted. "That's the brand, Grandpa. You're Grumpy Santa. Own it."

Red grumbled under his breath but adjusted his hat. Somewhere between late November and now, he'd stopped fighting. The kid was right—his sour mug and deadpan gripes had become the hook. And bookings *had* gone up. Snowberry Lodge wasn't at full capacity, but it wasn't bleeding red ink either.

"All right," he said. "Let's get it over with before my arthritis gets arthritis."

Benny spent a few minutes packing snowballs while Red did his best to calm Copper, who shifted and turned like he wanted it all to be over.

Once Benny had his phone ready, he held up a gloved hand and counted down on his fingers.

"Three...two...one—action!"

Red slouched dramatically on the driver's bench, the reins slack in his gloved hands.

"Welcome to Santa's winter fortress," he started, making his voice extra low and gravelly as he turned to look at the fort. "Marvel at the majestic walls of...slush.

Built by overpaid elves who apparently flunked architecture."

All of a sudden, he felt the cold punch rushing at him, a *thwump* on his chest, almost hard enough to take his breath away. At least it wasn't his face.

Red scowled. "And now the elves have resorted to violence. Perfect."

Benny scrambled, and in seconds, another snowball came flying but it was wider. It missed Red by a few feet but smashed into the crooked wall of the fort, making the structure slump with a satisfying *whoosh*.

Copper jerked at the sound, snorting clouds into the frosty air. His hooves stamped nervously.

"Easy, boy," Red murmured, tightening the reins.

But Benny was on a roll. He darted closer, heaving another snowball. This one clipped Copper's flank before exploding in a spray of powder.

The gelding startled hard, jerking sideways.

"Benny!" Red barked, but he had his face in that daggum cell phone!

Copper pranced, muscles bunching. His ears pinned back, and in the next breath, he lunged forward. The sleigh jolted, runners biting into the snowpack. Red clutched the reins with both hands, his stomach dropping.

"Grandpa!"

As Copper surged straight past the fort, Benny managed to scramble up to the bench, barely slinging himself next to Red.

"I'm so sorry! I didn't mean—"

"Don't apologize, just hang on!" Red yanked the reins, but Copper was blind with panic now, his breath pumping white clouds.

He headed straight for the frozen creek.

"No!" Red yanked the reins, but it was a wasted effort. Copper's hooves thundered, then slammed into the creek bed rocking the sleigh, and making the horse even more frenzied.

With indescribable strength, Copper rose up and stormed forward, banging the sleigh over ice and rocks, bringing it up the slippery banks to the edge of the wide, flat meadow beyond.

"Copper!" Red snapped the reins again, but that merely spurred on the animal.

He tore forward over the untouched crust, with the sleigh bouncing behind him. Benny squealed, clutching Red's arm.

"Grandpa!"

"Hang on!" Red hollered, using all his strength to yank back the reins. "Just stay low, Benny!"

The meadow spread wide, dazzling white. The runners hit logs and rocks, sliding on icy stones, the old metal tested. Red peered ahead, knowing full well what was at the other end of this stretch—the steep hill, sharp and unforgiving. If Copper didn't stop, they'd be dragged straight toward it.

"Whoa, boy!" Red bellowed. His voice tore at his throat. "Easy! Easy now!"

But the horse was wild-eyed, nostrils flaring, ears deaf

to commands. And Benny's bravado and maturity melted into terrified screams, muffled into Red's jacket.

"We'll be okay, boy!" Red growled the words he did not believe, his hands aching on the reins. "Look at me, Benny." His voice shook, but he forced it steady and stole a glance at his great-grandson. "You're all right. You hear me? You're safe. He's gotta run it off."

The boy's tear-bright eyes lifted. He nodded, trembling.

Red gritted his teeth and hauled again, pulling Copper's head to the side. The horse skidded, hooves spraying snow, momentum carrying them in a long arc across the meadow.

For one awful second Red thought they'd tip—the sleigh leaning, runner digging—but it thudded flat again. Copper lunged on, angling straight toward the far ridge.

"Not that way," Red muttered, tugging with every ounce of strength left in him. "Not today."

Copper stumbled, then found his footing. His ears flicked—at last listening to commands.

Finally—*finally*—Copper slowed, foam flecking his bit. His chest heaved, great clouds of steam rising into the frigid air. Red wrenched him to a halt, the sleigh jerking so hard both of them nearly pitched off the bench.

And it was over. Nothing but a panting beast, a whimpering child, and Red's poor heart walloping his chest. For a long, long moment, no one moved.

Then Benny hiccupped a sob. "Grandpa, I'm so sorry. I'm so sorry."

"'Sokay. We're okay. We just need help, 'cause the sleigh's pretty messed up."

Benny moaned. "I lost the phone," he wailed. "I dropped it when I jumped in the sleigh."

Red huffed out a breath and looked back to where they'd been—a half mile of drifts and snowbanks that would hide that phone until late spring.

How would they get home? Maybe they could take turns riding Copper, but he doubted the spooked old horse would stand for that. How would they get over the creek?

How long would they be out here, frozen and scared?

The meadow stretched silent around them, the hill's drop just yards away. Copper stood quivering, sides heaving. Benny pressed into Red's chest, clutching him like a lifeline.

Red felt tears sting his eyes—hot against the icy wind.

"We'll be all right," he whispered, mostly for Benny, maybe a little for himself. "We'll be all right."

But he didn't quite believe it. Not yet.

Red stroked the boy's back, trying to steady his own breathing. But then he saw Copper shifting, favoring his front right leg. Not bad, not broken, but the horse kept lifting it, pawing the air like the weight of the harness was too much.

"Blast it," Red muttered. "He's strained himself."

Benny looked up, wide-eyed. "What do we do?"

Red's gut clenched. Jack was the one who always handled the harnessing with quick hands and mastery of the skill. Red had learned the basics, sure, but he hadn't unharnessed a horse in years. He eyed the heavy traces, the straps cutting dark lines across Copper's coat. The animal trembled, breaking Red's heart.

"We get him loose," Red said, though his voice came out rough. "If he pulls with that leg like this, he could do real damage. He needs to walk it off a bit."

Benny scrambled down into the snow with him, hovering close but careful.

Red fumbled at the first buckle, his fingers clumsy in thick gloves. "Come on, now," he gritted. "Jack makes this look easy."

The strap finally gave with a snap, loosening just enough that Copper shook his head. Red moved to the next, yanking with frozen fingers, shoulders screaming from the strain of the ride.

The gelding stamped again, jerking sideways. The sleigh rocked. Red swore under his breath, bracing his knee against Copper for leverage as he worked the last buckle free. The leather had stiffened in the cold, fighting him every inch.

"There," he muttered, tugging the final trace loose.

The instant Copper felt the slack, he surged. Red had just enough time to stumble back, pulling Benny out of the way as the horse tore free of the shafts. Snow sprayed in a white burst as he bolted.

But not toward the lodge, not even toward the creek or the woods.

Red's heart dropped to his boots as Copper charged across the rest of the open meadow, straight toward the steep slope at the ridge.

"No," Red rasped, breath fogging. "No, no, *no*."

Beside him, Benny gasped. "Grandpa! He's running down the hill!"

Red could only watch, frozen, as Copper disappeared over the edge.

For the first time since the day he held his lifeless wife in his arms, Red Starling felt utterly lost and terrified.

Chapter Sixteen

Cindy squinted at the invoice on her desk, wishing she had better reading glasses...and a *much* better bank account.

Well, that would change with Henry's contract, which should show up any day now. He said he wanted to "land the plane" before Christmas, and that was in a week, so...*let's land it, Henry.*

She'd clicked her mouse to check her email when she heard the kitchen door open and felt a chill spread through the whole first floor. At the sound of a number of voices—some unfamiliar, one Jack's, and one MJ's—she rose to see if they needed help.

Coming around the corner to the kitchen, she saw a couple and two kids, all bundled in parkas and knit hats. They were laughing, their breath fogging in the air, stamping snow off their boots as they unwrapped scarves.

Jack was in carriage gear with his old-fashioned wool coat, the top hat off for the moment, standing in the mudroom with MJ, deep in conversation.

"Hello, everyone," she greeted the guests warmly. "All ready for a sleigh ride?"

"We're waiting for Santa," one of the kids said. "And a sleigh."

Cindy turned as Jack walked over to her, his expression hesitant. He came closer, leaning in to murmur, "The sleigh's not here."

Cindy blinked. "Where is it?"

"I let Red take it. Benny begged. They promised they'd be back with plenty of time." Jack's voice was calm, but his eyes carried something sharper—unease.

She glanced at the guests, happily chatting among themselves, patiently waiting for their scheduled ride.

"Did you call Red?" she asked.

"It's going straight to voicemail."

From the back, MJ produced a tray of goodies. "Cookies by the Christmas tree," she sang out. "And while you wait, I'll make hot cocoa with marshmallows." She beamed at the smaller child. "Do you like marshmallows?"

"I want to meet Grumpy Santa and go on that sleigh," he said.

Cindy frowned, wondering why so many guests said that about Santa. Was Red that grouchy to everyone? He hated the Santa gig, and Cindy knew it. But enough to not show for a ride, and take the sleigh?

The guests followed MJ like ducklings, drawn by the promise of food and warmth. Cindy leaned closer to Jack.

"Do you think something happened or he's just on strike?" she asked.

Jack shook his head. "I don't know, but it's not like

either of them. Red has bluster—it's part of his act. But Benny's the most reliable kid I know."

True enough. Something wasn't right.

MJ reappeared, giving Cindy a look that managed to be both reassuring and worried. "Gracie's on her way home. I'll call her to see if she's heard something from them," she said quietly, squeezing Cindy's arm.

"Let's grab the UTV and go look," Jack said. "Come with me, Cin."

Cindy nodded, hurrying to the mudroom to get her coat.

They crossed the snow toward the carport, agreeing to stop in the ski shed to see what Nicole knew. Jack's strides were long and decisive, but she felt the pulse of tension rolling off him.

Nicole was inside her store, just finishing up with two men renting skis, thanking them for their business.

She took one look at Cindy, then Jack, and her smile faded.

"What's wrong?" she asked, coming out from behind the counter.

"Did you see Dad and Benny leave?" Cindy asked.

Nicole frowned, looking toward the large display window. "Yeah. An hour ago? A little more? They were laughing. Benny was bouncing in the sleigh like it was the best day of his life. Why? What's wrong?"

"They should have been back thirty minutes ago," Jack said. "And Red's not picking up his phone."

"Really?"

Cindy forced calm into her tone. "We're going to take

the UTV and check around. MJ has the guests. Gracie's on her way."

"What can I do?"

"Call Cindy if you see or hear anything," Jack said. "We'll find them, don't worry. We'll find them."

Holding hope from the determined tone in his voice, Cindy went with him to the utility vehicle they used in much better weather. The old snowmobile had died a few years ago and Cindy had wanted to buy another, but...they were expensive, and she had put it off.

Now, she regretted that decision.

"You think this can get us over the trails?" she asked as they hopped in.

"The short trail, not over the creek or..." He closed his eyes. "I wish I hadn't agreed to let them leave without me."

"Don't blame yourself, Jack," she said, yanking on her seatbelt. "Take the main trail as far as we can, then get help if we don't see them."

Snow sprayed behind the UTV as the old beast rumbled forward, Jack's jaw set with a whole host of emotions Cindy couldn't read. The wind burned her cheeks, and her heart thudded like a drum.

"I should tell you something," Jack shouted over the engine. "About Benny."

Cindy narrowed her eyes against the wind. "What about him?"

"He's under the impression that if he saves the lodge, you'll get him a puppy."

Her breath caught. "*What?* I never said that—"

"You kind of did, though you might not realize it," Jack said grimly. "And he's holding onto it. He thinks if he does something big, heroic...you'll make good on the promise."

Is that why he and Red hadn't come back yet? "Well, how is he going to do that?"

"TikTok videos."

"What?"

"He's turned 'Grumpy Santa' into a thing on social media and he's the one responsible for all the business and sleigh rides."

Cindy's jaw dropped. "That's why people are all calling Red 'grumpy'?" She choked a laugh. "Benny did... wait, how? He's not allowed—"

Jack pointed toward the thick pine trees. "Maybe they went back to that snow hut down by the creek."

She followed his gaze, but it was impossible to see from here.

"I hope not," she said. "The creek always spooks Copper. I know that—but did Red?"

"Look! Are those runner marks from the sleigh?" Jack asked, rumbling the UTV in toward the small turn-off.

"Yes," she said. "But the UTV can't go very far down there."

"I'll go on foot, then." He brought the UTV to a stop and they unbuckled in perfect unison, jumping out and hustling to meet at the front of the vehicle.

"I know this meadow," Jack said, bracing against the cold. "There's a steep side of the mountain on the other end. I hope—"

"Jack. Look!" She put her hand over her mouth, just as something moved well beyond the trees.

He saw it, too, and they both darted in that direction, passing a crumbled remnant of a snow fort and—

"There they are!" In the distance, two figures huddled in the back seat of the sleigh, both wrapped in Red's heavy coat. But Copper was gone.

Relief and terror tangled in Cindy's chest as she scanned the treeline, the ridge, the shadows along the slope for the horse. "He must have gone down the side."

Swearing under his breath, Jack turned to her, grabbing her shoulders. "Go get Nicole. Bring skis. Hurry. I'll go get them."

Her heart slammed against her ribs. "Jack—"

"Go!"

With that, he took off toward Benny and Red. Cindy pivoted and ran back to the UTV, the engine growling as she gunned it back toward the lodge.

The ride back was a blur. Snow slapped her face, stinging her eyes, but she barely noticed.

What would they have done without Jack? He moved on all cylinders and loved her family as much...as much as she loved him.

How could she doubt him?

She practically flew off the ground as she came up the last hill before the lodge, slipping and sliding toward the shed. Nicole ran out before she turned the engine off.

"Get skis and let's go!" Cindy hollered.

"Skis?"

"Copper went down the hill on the other side of the meadow."

"With the sleigh?" she asked, horrified.

"No, no. They unharnessed him and he—"

Nicole didn't let her finish. She leaped into action, ready to do whatever she could to help the family she loved.

Chapter Seventeen
Nicole

The UTV rattled like it hated every inch of the climb, tires spinning wildly before catching with a bone-jarring jolt that slammed Nicole's teeth together. She clung to the cold steel bar above her head, her fingers stiff and cold despite the gloves she wore.

Next to her, Mom hunched over the wheel, jaw set in grim determination, as though she could will the machine into conquering the snow-covered trail. Wind tore through the open sides, sharp as broken glass.

"Jack texted while you got the gear," Mom shouted over the growling engine. "They're okay, but Copper's definitely down the slope. He's okay, but...far."

He was not okay, Nicole thought. He was terrified and alone and probably about to panic run and get completely lost.

Nicole grunted and dropped her head back, barely able to breathe. *Copper.* Her boy. Her partner.

The UTV veered sideways again, tires hunting for a grip on the rutted track. Snow sprayed the windshield in sheets. Nicole pressed a hand hard to her chest, as if she could stop it from bursting out of her.

"Did you know about this Grumpy Santa thing?" Nicole shouted over the engine.

"Did you?" She threw a look. "Jack just told me on the way up here."

"One of the guests waiting for the sleigh told me after you left. I went over to see if everyone was okay and they told me that they—and many others—have been following this account. Benny must have made it!"

"He did." Somehow, Mom managed a dry laugh. "He decided that if he saved our December, he'd get a dog for Christmas."

Nicole just closed her eyes, overwhelmed with love and worry.

"Well, I think he did," she said. "I jumped on the account and there are *thousands* of followers. So I posted an announcement—hashtag *grumpysantaismissing*. I thought maybe people would know where they are—or pray."

"We could use all the help." Her mother fought the spinning wheels again, and the UTV crested a rise and lurched to a shuddering stop near Moose Creek. Nicole didn't even want to look beyond the treeline to the ridge. She knew that drop.

"They're back there," Mom said, pointing. "On the other side of the creek."

Between the trees, the creek shimmered like a scar of broken glass, ice cracked and jagged where the sleigh had gone through. Beyond, the snow stretched for what felt like a mile, but Nicole knew it wasn't.

But at the other side, the slope plunged steep, a ridge

of pines and stones and…no real trail. It was as close to back-country skiing as Nicole had ever done or ever thought she would do.

At one time, she could do a groomed black diamond if she had to. But that? That was rugged, loaded with trees, and would challenge an expert.

But…*Copper*.

Dad came running, snow flying at his boots, his face pale and hard. "You made it."

Her mother staggered out of the vehicle, grabbing a mountain of blankets. Nicole leapt after her, boots sinking to her calves in powder as she reached for her ski equipment.

"Are they okay?" Nicole's voice cracked as she peered through the trees.

"Red's keeping Benny calm by the sleigh. They're freezing. I've got to get them warm." His eyes landed on the skis in Nicole's hands. "Where are mine?"

"I didn't bring them." She lifted her chin, defiant even as her body trembled. "Benny and Red need you to get them back to the UTV. You're stronger than I am. I'll get Copper."

Jack's mouth flattened. "Nic—"

"Don't argue. I know how to handle him in a crisis."

For a beat, his eyes bored into hers, fury and fear warring. Then his shoulders sagged, and the fury cracked into something more fragile. "Are you sure you can handle that slope?"

Nicole snapped her goggles down. "Never been so sure."

Mom stepped in. "Nicole, are you—"

"Mom, Dad, please. I can do this."

They shared a parental look and gave up the fight at the same moment. It was the mountain, she knew, that would put up the real battle.

The creek ice groaned under their boots as Mom tottered, Jack steadying her with a hand at her elbow. Under Nicole's arms, her skis and boots clattered, every muscle thrumming with adrenaline.

They reached the sleigh, which looked no worse for the wear, to be honest. But Benny's face was blotchy and wet, cheeks flaming against the cold, his sobs ragged in the frozen air. Red held him tight, massive mittened hands dwarfing the little boy's small fingers.

Mom dropped into the sleigh, wrapping the blankets around both of them and tucking Benny against her chest. "I've got you, baby. You're safe."

Jack got blankets on Red, covering the old man while Nicole snapped on her ski boots

"Listen, Nic," Jack said. "Copper's scared but not hurt. I saw him, and God willing he's still at the bottom of the slope. You can get him."

The confidence in his voice made her feel like invincible eight-year-old Nicole Kessler, who wasn't afraid of snow or trees or steep, steep runs.

She dropped her skis to the snow. The sound of the bindings snapping shut under her boots jolted something deep inside her chest. *Snap.* Old muscle memory fired awake.

Jack stepped forward, his voice low, urgent. "Just—don't kill yourself."

She gave a dry laugh. "Best advice you ever gave me, Dad. Meet us on the old Aspen View trail. Five bucks says I'll beat you there."

His eyes flickered. "I'll take that bet, girl."

With that, she pushed off and didn't look back. Her entire world had narrowed to one reason to ski: Copper.

The slope fell away like a white wall. Trees dotted the incline, their limbs black and sharp as claws...their wells deep and deadly.

But it was probably the trees and rocks that saved Copper, who stood like a small chestnut speck at the bottom where the old trail passed. All alone and scared to death.

Not for long, buddy. Here I come.

Nicole shoved off.

The first rush nearly stole her breath. Gravity yanked her forward, skis biting the snow with a scrape that rattled up her bones. Her legs wobbled. Terror clawed at her throat, screaming at her to fall, to slow, to stop.

Eyes ahead. Where you look is where you go.

Her father's voice snapped clean and steady in her head while her gaze shifted from the next ten feet in front of her to the horse she'd loved for ten years.

She leaned into the first turn, tipping her weight to her downhill ski. The edge carved, powder spraying her shin. Her poles rattled against the snow. She arced back the other way, then again, each S-turn a personal victory.

A tree lunged into her path, sudden and unexpected.

Pizza wedge. Toes in. Slow it down.

She forced her skis inward, edges biting deep. Her speed dropped. She righted herself, lungs searing, eyes watering, the tree behind her now, then another.

She turned, slowed, curved and let her skis eat the snow, her thighs and chest burning as she attacked every inch.

And then she heard Copper's neigh grow more desperate, loud enough to cut through any thoughts. Her head snapped up. His dark eyes locked onto hers, ears pitched forward, body trembling but still. Like he'd been waiting for her all this time.

This wasn't about her. It wasn't about the fall nineteen years ago, or the tree well, or the promise she'd made to herself to never put skis on again. This was about Copper.

Nicole bent lower, feeling the air slice against her goggles, her breath hot in the frozen mask. She tipped into another turn, smoother this time, feeling like the mountain obeyed her.

Yes. *Yes!* Her skis carved like they remembered. Her body found rhythm.

She heard her father's old encouragement echo through her head: *Flow with it. Trust the edges. The mountain isn't against you. It's under you.*

The fear dissolved into exhilaration. Wind rushed against her, sharp and wild. Powder flew in glittering arcs. The rhythm pulsed through her muscles: edge, carve, release. Edge, carve, release.

Copper's ears pricked higher. He neighed again, a sound full of recognition and hope.

"I'm coming, boy!" Nicole shouted, her own voice breaking into laughter.

A final sweep, a graceful whoosh, and she skidded to a stop in a spray of snow, right in front of him.

She dropped her poles and flung herself forward, arms wrapping around his thick neck. He trembled beneath her touch, warm breath gusting against her cheek.

"Oh, Copper. My boy." Her words cracked into a sob. She pulled out a sticky peppermint, fingers shaking, and he nibbled it from her palm, crunching with a snort.

She pressed her forehead to his mane. "We did it. You and me. We conquered our fears."

The walk to Aspen View trail felt endless, with Nicole's skis heavy under one arm, poles dragging, the other arm draped around Copper's neck.

She coaxed him step by step, murmuring encouragement. "Steady, boy. Just a little farther. We've got this."

When they turned the last bend to the old trail, she heard the rumble of the UTV and felt her frozen lips lift into a smile.

"Dang, he won that bet." She squeezed her horse. "We'll get him next time."

And there would be a next time, she knew, because she was a skier again, a thought that covered her in a wave of euphoria.

At the sight of her parents, huddled together on the UTV, more bliss washed over her—tinged with a bittersweet hope that somehow her family could be whole again.

Mom popped up at the sight of her, arms out, calling her name.

Her father jumped out and ran to her, somehow hugging her and the horse.

"Are they okay?" she asked. "Benny? Red? Are they—"

"They're fine. At the lodge, warm and safe. In a little trouble, but they're fine." He squeezed her and kissed her on the top of the head, his body vibrating as much as hers. "So proud of you, honey."

She smiled and leaned back, blinking back tears. "You were with me on every turn, Dad."

"But you didn't need me." He kissed her head again. "I love you, Nic."

"Love you, too," she murmured.

Mom joined them and the family hug, all of them wrapped together, the Kessler trio.

For the first time in years, Nicole felt whole. Not fractured, not afraid.

And though she didn't know how long it could last, right now it was enough. Enough to feel like this was the best moment of her life.

Chapter Eighteen

Red

Christmas Eve at Snowberry Lodge always had a hum to it, like the mountain itself was singing carols low and steady. Tonight, that hum filled Red's bones while he sat at the head of the long kitchen table, watching his clan finish off the last bites of MJ's prime rib and mashed potatoes.

Benny still wore his crooked tie from the school Christmas chorus event they'd all gone to earlier. Yes, it was just to watch him stand in the back row and move his mouth with all of them knowing full well their little "tech mogul" wasn't singing a thing.

But Red didn't care. He couldn't love that kid more, even if he faked singing carols at school.

He sure was singing now. Chirping about a puppy, about how his idea saved the day, and—of course—how the video he'd just uploaded already had three thousand likes.

He passed around his mother's phone, who had reluctantly let him use it. She'd promised to get another phone for Red, but he was perfectly happy without that stinking thing weighing down his pocket.

"You gotta look, Grandpa!" Benny exclaimed after

Nicole watched and gave her approval, then handed the phone to Red.

He squinted at the screen. Oh, there he was sitting in the sleigh this afternoon, beard frosted with snow. At his ten-year-old director's insistence, Red dropped the grumpy act—as much as possible—to deliver a heartfelt message about love, peace, and the birth of baby Jesus.

"How do you like that?" he said. "I didn't have to beg anyone to come and visit."

"Because we're booked," Cindy said with a smile.

"You saved December, Benny," MJ said, reaching to smooth his hair. "We were scraping the bottom, and now look at us. Every room and cabin reserved through New Year's."

Gracie, arms folded, still shook her head and tsked at him, though there was no heat in it anymore. "Ten years old and running social media campaigns behind your mother's back? What am I facing when you're sixteen?"

"Oh, he'll be the CEO of a company by then," Jack joked.

Benny tried to look contrite but couldn't stop grinning. "Worked, didn't it?"

"Yes," Gracie admitted with a sigh, then whispered, "but next time, you *and Grandpa* should ask first."

Red snorted. "Won't be a next time. I'm retiring from that job."

All the faces around the table turned to him with a chorus of, "What?" and "You can't quit!" and "You're Grumpy Santa forever!"

He waved it all off, knowing deep in his heart...they would win.

Benny was up on his knees now, leaning over the table to look at Cindy. "So, ahem, Aunt Cindy. About that puppy..."

She raised both brows with mock surprise. "Puppy? I don't know what you're talking about, sweetheart."

Red sipped his coffee to hide the chuckle. She was lying smoother than fresh ice, because he knew for a fact that little teddy bear-looking mutt was sleeping in Jack's cabin right now. The whole family did—except Benny.

The moment was warm as mulled cider, until Jack pushed back from the table. "Well, I hate to break this up, but I need to head out."

Silence dipped around them. He'd warned them plenty that Christmas Eve was his end date. Vermont called, and, more specifically, his mother.

Nicole made a face. "I hate that you won't be here tomorrow, Dad."

"I do, too, honey. But the red-eye out of Salt Lake will get me back to Burlington in time to make Bertie's Christmas brunch at the retirement center. I gave her my word I'd be there."

They all started to get up and begin a round of hugs, high-fives, and goodbyes. Red noticed Cindy pick up a platter and step away toward the island, then slip out the mudroom door.

His heart hurt for her, so he covered by standing up, too, while they all wished Jack well and thanked him for the sleigh rides.

"I'll walk you out, Jack," Red said.

Benny piped up, "Can I—"

"Nope," Red cut in. "Finish your pie."

The two men stepped out into the hush of Christmas Eve snow, neither bothering with jackets for the short walk to Cabin One. Flakes sifted soft as powdered sugar, settling on their shoulders. The air bit sharp but clean, and the glow from the lodge windows spilled over the yard.

Jack jammed his hands into his pants pockets. "You don't have to see me off, Red."

"I do, though." Red motioned toward the cabins. "Besides, I need to check on a certain four-legged surprise."

Jack's mouth twitched. "He's curled up by the wood-stove in his crate. Benny's gonna flip."

They crunched along the path, boots squeaking on snowpack. They made small talk—about reservations, how full the sleigh rides had been, even about Jack's mother, who apparently ruled her retirement community back East like a benevolent monarch.

"She's the Christmas queen," Jack said with a shrug. "Organizes carols, makes sure no one's alone. I owe it to her to be there tomorrow."

Red nodded but couldn't help the memory hitting hard—Jack leaving once before, on Christmas, walking away from Cindy and Nicole to do his fancy TV job.

"You sure this just isn't you making the same mistake twice?" Red asked, his voice low because he hated that he had to ask.

Jack stopped, blinking at some snowflakes that fell on his lashes. "It's different. Back then, I had my priorities screwed up. This time, I'm just going home for Christmas."

"Mmm." Red slowed his step. "And Cindy?"

Jack exhaled that breath hard, steam fogging the night. "Well, I asked her if we could..." He grunted. "She doesn't want to try again. It's that simple."

Red eyed him. "You asked her?"

Jack nodded. "I did, but she was just dead silent. She might say she's forgiven me—and she might really think she has—but deep inside? I don't think she trusts me not to leave again."

"So don't."

Jack gave a soft laugh. "Easier said than done."

"Is it?" Red pressed. "I know you have a life in Vermont."

"Not much of one," he muttered.

"And your mother."

"Who might not notice I'm here or..." He gave Red a hopeful look. "Might want to come back here with me. Park City was her home until my dad decided he wanted to 'retire' in Vermont, which made no sense. Now he's gone and if I were..." His voice trailed off. "Doesn't matter, Red. Cindy's moved on, built a life. Nicole, too. They don't need me."

Red rooted for the words to tell him how very wrong he was. But Jack was sixty years old—a grown man who didn't need his former father-in-law telling him he was a fool.

"Are you sure of that?" Red asked, hoping to get Jack to see straight.

"I'm sure that I don't know how to tell Cindy how I feel and what I want. I just don't know how to tell her."

The man's voice cracked, and for once, Red saw not the smooth talker, not the championship athlete or the ESPN commentator, but just a man who loved a woman and had probably never stopped.

Red clapped a heavy hand on his shoulder. "Son, you don't need a sales pitch. You don't need perfect timing. You just tell her. Straight as skis downhill. You love her, you say so. You want your family back, you say so. Cindy deserves that kind of honesty."

Jack swallowed. "You make it sound easy."

"'Cause it is. Hardest part's stepping up. The rest is her call."

They reached the cabin porch. Warm light glowed through the crack in the curtain. Red paused, letting the words hang.

Jack dragged a hand through his hair. "For what it's worth, Red—I want to be a family again. I'm still in love with her. I always was and always will be. I love Cindy the way I did the day I married her. I just don't know how to tell her."

The cabin door creaked open, making them realize it hadn't been fully closed.

Cindy stood there, cheeks flushed from the fire inside, cradling a bundle of light brown curls that squirmed in her arms. She'd clearly been tending to the pup, but her gaze was fixed on Jack, steady and unwavering.

"You just did," she said softly.

Jack froze.

Red's heart gave a satisfied thump. He stepped back into the snow, leaving the porch to them. "Guess my work here's done," he muttered, turning toward the lodge lights.

Behind him, the puppy yipped, Jack stammered, and he heard Cindy laugh, sounding a lot like that girl on the day she married Jack Kessler.

What do you know? Maybe Christmas still had a miracle or two up its sleeve.

Chapter Nineteen

Cindy hadn't meant to eavesdrop. She'd only opened the cabin door because the puppy fidgeted like a live wire in her arms and needed to go outside. But then she heard Jack say he loved her the way he did the day they got married—he *loved* her.

The words landed like a lit match in her chest, catching on old kindling.

Now, in the hush that followed, the tiny puppy wiggled and wormed, a warm bundle of teddy-bear fluff that smelled faintly of the fireplace he'd been sleeping next to.

Her father had muttered something and disappeared into the darkness, leaving them alone. Jack blinked at her, snow caught in his lashes, looking suddenly twenty-five and hopeful.

She pressed the puppy into his coat so she'd have an excuse to break eye contact, then laughed when the little guy climbed up and tried to chew his ear.

"He likes you," she managed.

"Poor thing has no taste."

She smiled up at him. "I don't agree."

He looked at her for a moment, then sighed. "Come in for a minute?"

She nodded. "Gimme a second." She glanced at the puppy, using him as an excuse, but really, she needed air more than the little guy needed to find his favorite patch of snow.

Setting him on the ground, she took a deep breath and centered herself.

Jack still loved her. What did that mean? Where did that leave them? Guess she was about to find out.

Scooping up the puppy, she went back into the cabin. In the warm glow from the fireplace, she could see the emotions playing over Jack's handsome features—a little fear, a little hope, a lot of...yes, love.

His declaration still echoed in her head, louder than the tick of the baseboard heater and the snuffle sounds the puppy made when she put him into his cozy little crate.

On the bed, Jack's suitcase gaped open, folded shirts packed neatly, next to a row of sweaters she'd seen him wear these past few weeks.

"Déjà vu," she said softly, sinking to the edge of the bed. "Christmas, an open suitcase, and you flying out into the cold."

He winced, then sat beside her, the mattress dipping in a familiar way for two people who'd shared a bed for twenty years.

"It isn't the same, Cin."

"No," she said. "We're not the same."

They weren't. Ten years had left tracks—a lighter

silver at Jack's temples that looked unfairly handsome, tiny lines fanning from her eyes that no cream could erase, and a steadiness in her that had been forged by holding life together with lists and grit and a smile.

They had learned how to live with the ache without letting divorce define them, she supposed. But being strong was not the same as being whole.

Jack sighed heavily. "I should have said those words ten years ago," he murmured. "I should have said a lot of things."

"Me, too," she said. "We were both stubborn and stupid and..."

"Mostly stupid," he finished. "At least I was. You wanted a husband who put family before work, and you were one hundred percent right."

She just shook her head, really not wanting to use their last few minutes together to rehash a decision they'd made a decade ago.

Jack cleared his throat and turned to her. "I asked once and you..."

"Were rendered speechless," she said. "If you took that as rejection, I'm sorry."

His dark eyes flickered. "It wasn't?"

She shook her head.

"Then I'll ask again, Cin. Could there be a future?" He closed his eyes, clearly not happy with what he'd just said. "It sounds clumsy and cliché, which it is, but I don't know how else to approach this. It's not a movie—we can't kiss and let the camera pan to the moon and a second happy ever after. We have lives to undo—but I would, Cindy." He leaned closer. "I would like to try again. At least to talk about it and explore options."

She had promised herself a thousand times that if this moment came, she'd be resolute. Hard line. All or nothing. No more half-promises and hopeful maybe's that could blow away with the first strong wind.

But here he was, the father of her daughter, the man she had once loved with easy certainty, offering the only thing an honest person could—not a guarantee, but a beginning.

"Yes," she whispered. "I think...we could...explore options."

Whatever *that* meant.

He went very still, and then his hand found hers on the bedspread. His fingers were cold from the walk, his palm callused from weeks of handling those reins. He'd given up nearly a month of his life to fix the problem in hers.

And she'd fallen right back in love with him.

"Why don't we consider something after the holidays?" he said. "Maybe in spring. It's quieter here. I'll come back and we could...we could give it—give *us*—the space we deserve. We'd take it slow, but it would be real."

Maybe in spring. Maybe. The word echoed, gentle and maddening. Her heart had wanted now. Not a boy's daydream, but a man's decision.

But he was leaving. Because he'd promised his mother, because he was a good son, because life wasn't a fairytale, and planes didn't wait for better timing.

"Spring," she said, trying to sound brave. "We can start there."

His thumb moved over the ridge of her knuckles. He didn't lean in. She didn't either. The not-kiss hovered between them like a snowflake that never landed, beautiful and cold.

His phone chimed—a little digital bell that, absurdly, made the puppy lift his head. Jack glanced down. "My ride's here."

"Of course it is." She stood first, because if she didn't, she might ask him not to go, and that wouldn't be fair to either of them.

She found his scarf and looped it around his neck, her fingers brushing his throat, the intimacy of the motion punching through ten years of distance. "Come on. I'll walk you."

She waited while he zipped the suitcase, donned a jacket, and took a final look around the cabin. After all that, he leaned over the crate.

"G'bye, little roommate. Hope Benny gives you a good name."

They stepped out into a hushed night, lit by the colored lights all over the evergreen trees. The Uber idled in front of the lodge, headlights casting a pale runway down the snow-packed drive.

In the kitchen window, she caught movement—probably MJ doing the dinner clean-up.

A few feet from the car, Jack stopped and put his suitcase down. He wrapped his arms around her and held on.

She held her breath for…something. A promise, a date, a confirmation, a kiss.

"Safe flight," she said into his coat.

"Merry Christmas, Cinnie."

The old, most intimate nickname that he only used when they were alone, cut deeper than the goodbye.

He turned quickly when they parted, but she could have sworn she saw tears in his eyes.

He stepped to the car, opened the door, lifted a hand, and then climbed in.

A moment later, the taillights slid down toward the road and vanished past the pines. The sound of tires on hardpack faded until there was only the wind and her breath.

The first time he'd left at Christmas, she'd watched in shock, the moment making her heart feel like a glass dropped in slow motion, then shattered.

Tonight, she watched with eyes wide open and felt the sting in her throat that was merely a mix of grief and hope tangled together like knotted Christmas light strings.

As the car lights disappeared, she went back up to his cabin. Once Benny had gone home with Gracie and Red, she'd bring little No Name into the lodge for the night.

Inside, she let the warmth hold her, checking on the sleeping puppy.

Unable to resist, she sat on Jack's bed again, feeling the sting of tears. Turning, she reached for one of his pillows and put her face in it, inhaling the familiar scent of pine and soap and her husband.

And she cried like the first time he left her, until all the tears were gone.

Much later, Cindy was surprised to find MJ still at the sink and cleaning up when she walked back into the mudroom.

"You sure are slow without me," she said, kicking off her boots. "Where is everyone?"

MJ eyed her. "Gracie and Red went back up to their house to get Benny in bed, although good luck with that on Christmas Eve. Didn't you see them?"

She shook her head. "I was with the puppy in Jack's— in Cabin One. In fact, if everyone's gone, I'll go get him now." She looked down at the boots she'd just shed.

"Wait." MJ came closer, holding her dishtowel, searching Cindy's face. "You've been crying."

Cindy smiled. "You know I love a good Christmas goodbye."

"Oh, hon. C'mere." She put her arm around Cindy and walked her into the kitchen. "We'll get the dog in a minute. You need some love."

"I'm fine."

MJ rolled her eyes. "There's a little wine left. Want some?"

Cindy nodded and, a minute later, they were at the table with two glasses of red between them.

"So, how was it?" MJ finally asked.

Cindy shrugged. "He asked if we could maybe try again."

Her sister drew back, sucking in a breath. "And you said..."

"Yes, but—"

"Yes, but nothing! You two belong together!"

Did they belong together? Then why did "maybe in spring" feel like such an empty promise? Cindy ran her palm along the table, feeling the familiar nicks in the pine. "It was...nice. It's just—"

"Not quite enough," MJ finished for her.

"Not tonight, anyway." Cindy took a deep drink of wine, which was sharp and earthy in her mouth. "I wanted...I don't know. A thing you can't realistically ask for. Not at our age. Not with our history."

"You wanted him to plant a flag." MJ leaned back, studying her with nothing but wisdom in her crystal blue eyes. "I get it."

Cindy exhaled and managed a small laugh. "He didn't even kiss me."

"Fool," MJ said, but without heat. "Maybe that's wise. Maybe it means he's serious. Waiting for the right..." She tipped her head, listening. "Did you hear that? Did a car just pull up?"

Cindy heard the sharp *thunk* of a car door shutting out front, unable to stop her gasp of hope.

"He's back," she whispered, reaching for MJ's hand, hope rising up in her. "He knows that was a lackluster goodbye and he's back. He did say he loves me and I never..." She pushed out of her chair, her heart clobbering the underside of her ribs.

MJ caught Cindy's arm as she got up. "Wait."

"Wait?" Cindy choked. "That's all I've done for ten years."

"Just wait," MJ insisted. "Do not fling yourself onto him like a golden retriever who's been left alone for five minutes. He can do the work of saying it twice."

"He already said it once," Cindy whispered, but she paused, her pulse pounding in her throat.

She could see the whole moment unfolding in her imagination...Jack on the porch with snow in his hair, breathless words about not being able to leave on Christmas again, the kiss he hadn't given her because he was, yes, a fool.

"I'll get the door," MJ said, then wiped her hands, smoothed her hair, and headed down the hall.

Cindy followed, but hovered in the archway, closing her eyes to listen to the greeting. What would MJ say? What would—

"Hello." Her sister sounded pleasant and puzzled. "I'm sorry, I know you...give me a second...your name is—?"

"Henry Lassiter."

Cindy slapped her hand against her chest, shocked.

"Ms. Kess—Cindy—invited me. I apologize for the late hour, but I thought I might catch her. It's not too late, is it?"

At eight o'clock on Christmas Eve? Cindy frowned,

trying to handle the physical ache of disappointment in her gut.

It didn't matter. Jack hadn't returned, and she had to handle this.

Taking a breath, she breezed down the hall to the entryway, catching MJ's expression as she turned. To her surprise, her sister's features had gone still, her color shifting from creamy pink to...blanched gray.

Cindy stepped into the foyer. "Henry. I didn't expect you...tonight."

"You did invite me." His smile was fast and bright, the kind that had probably opened a thousand doors. "I'm sorry for the holiday timing, but it's critical that we get the paperwork into process this week. There are some very advantageous considerations if we formally file before the new year, but we need a certain number of business days. Time is tight. May I come in?"

He didn't quite wait for the response, stepping inside with his overcoat open as he wiped his feet on the mat.

"Five minutes, max," he added with a smile as he made his way into the great room.

Cindy started to follow, but turned to her silent and shocked sister to make the appropriate introduction—these two hadn't even met yet—but MJ was shaking her head, her eyes wide.

"What's the—"

MJ held up both hands and shot off to the kitchen, leaving Cindy's jaw open. Why would she do that?

Henry cleared his throat to get her attention.

She turned to find him at the antique credenza under

the window, a leather portfolio open. He extracted a sheaf of crisp papers and a pen.

All around him, Christmas had the room lit to a soft glow—the lights still glimmering on the tree, and more outside the darkened window glass, the fire settled into friendly embers.

Everything felt a little...odd. The fact that he'd come now, his rushed style, his lack of even acknowledging MJ.

"Here's the agreement exactly as we discussed," he said, with no preamble or small talk. "I put in two hundred fifty thousand by year's end, and you transfer the fifty into the investment account now. That's returned to you with the first draw, before January first. From a tax standpoint, that timing is hugely beneficial. We just sign and initiate the transfer tonight, and every-thing's in place. Easy."

"It's Christmas Eve," she said, her voice raspy.

"I know, but we need five business days to avoid massive and so-unnecessary taxes. You've had enough of those this year, don't you think?" His voice was warm butter, his smile sheer confidence.

"But...it feels rushed."

"That's how these things are, Cindy." He angled his head in apology. "And it's on me, I'm afraid. I was stuck in New York far longer than I expected. I literally landed in Salt Lake an hour ago and came straight away. These things always go down to the wire. But let's get it signed and scanned."

He held out his pen.

"But...don't you want to...say hello to my sister?"

Cindy heard herself ask, stalling. "She's my partner. You'll need her signature."

"One will do, especially once we have the account loaded and ready. You'll be able to start the renovations in early January, and be booking the hikers for spring and summer." Henry tapped the line for her name. "You can sign anytime, of course, but this is the last window for the tax advantage. Sign here, we'll move that money, and we'll be done. You will have two hundred and fifty thousand more dollars before the end of the year."

Wasn't that what she'd started the holiday season wanting? No, she wanted the tax bill covered and Benny, of all unlikely people, accomplished that. But December's awesome income could not sustain them forever. This could.

She took a step closer, reaching for the black and gold pen he held. Mont Blanc, she thought absently as she closed her fingers around the expensive tool. It felt heavy and slick and final between her fingers.

"Cindy," MJ said from the doorway.

She froze, mostly at the icy tone packed into that one word. Turning, she looked at her sister, who clutched a book—one of the photo albums?—against her chest.

"Can I speak with you, please?"

"Of course, but let me introduce you to—"

"*Now.*"

Cindy shuddered at the tone, still gripping the pricey pen. Without even looking at Henry, she walked toward her sister, pulled out of the room by the sheer force of her insistence and the warning in her eyes.

"In the kitchen," MJ said, taking her there.

Cindy's heart pounded with each step, her lips closed as if she wasn't supposed to talk.

At the table, MJ dropped the photo album with a thud and flipped it open. Like every one of these stored in the hutch, the page had Polaroids pasted in with a name and a date underneath, creating a visual record of every guest who'd ever spent even a single night at the Snowberry Lodge.

Many of them included MJ's notes, like "Loves Cabin Three," and "Always wants extra blankets," and "They got engaged!"

"Didn't he look familiar to you?" MJ demanded.

Cindy drew back, remembering the sensation when she'd first met the man. "Yes, he did. I thought he reminded me of..." Her voice trailed off as she looked down at the open page and the picture MJ pointed to.

"Well, I never forget a face," MJ said. "The moment I saw him I knew he'd stayed here before. I couldn't place it with the suit and the haircut and the big-city polish but —look." She jabbed a finger at a Polaroid from eight winters ago. A man leaned against the porch rail in an old ski jacket, chin tucked into his scarf, his smile a shade less practiced but unmistakable.

The handwritten note beneath read:

Glen Avery...February 2017

And MJ's scribbled notes said: *Solo. Charming. Interested in local lodges.*

"Glen Avery?" Cindy stared at his face, knowing beyond a shadow of a doubt that he was the same man currently standing in her great room waiting for her to sign a contract...and transfer fifty thousand dollars to him.

All the blood drained from her head, making the room nearly spin.

"I did a search on Glen Avery's name," MJ continued, her voice sharp as steel. She held out her phone so Cindy could read the words, but they were just swimming, everything underwater.

The article headline finished the gut punch...

Big Elk Lodge in Sawtooth Mountains Swindled Out of Thousands, Forced to Close

There was a photo of him, attached to the story, the same smile, the same eyes, with a caption that read, "Glen Avery, consultant."

"He went to prison for five years and now he's out and doing the same thing." MJ ground out the words. "He must stay at these places all over the mountains and sniff out a victim."

Cindy's knees went a little watery. She braced on the counter, the relief so intense it left her lightheaded. She hadn't signed. She hadn't moved the money. She hadn't lost the lodge out of desperation and blind faith.

"Okay," she breathed. "Okay. I'll go tell him to leave right—"

The front door closed softly and they both gasped, hurrying out of the kitchen and down the hall.

They caught sight of the car lights heading out, and turned to see the great room completely empty, but one piece of paper must have fluttered to the floor when he rushed out.

MJ made a sound that was half victory, half fury.

"I'm so grateful for you, MJ," Cindy whispered. "You're usually the trusting one and I'm pragmatic." She bent over and picked up the agreement, which was just a page of legal gibberish she suspected meant nothing.

It was merely a trap to steal a lot of money, and she'd almost stepped right into it.

Tossing the pen on the table, she walked to the hearth and fed the page between the logs, watching the neat letters curl and blacken as the fire flickered back to life.

MJ stood behind her, one hand warm on her shoulder. "We'll figure it out," she said simply.

Cindy nodded and stepped away. "I better go get the puppy," she said softly. "I'll be back."

MJ didn't offer to go with her, probably understanding she needed to be alone. In the mudroom, she grabbed her jacket and that stupid red hat and slipped them on, walking out into the stillness of the Christmas-lit night.

She looked at the two sets of car tracks—Henry's and Jack's—and fought the urge to get a little dramatic over how those two men just rode right over her second chances.

Well, they did. And she needed to get out of her fairytale dreams and go back to pragmatic and sensible. That worked better for Cindy Kessler.

She took a few steps and paused at the sleigh,

reaching out to jingle one of the bells, the sound taking her heart for a ride.

Taking a breath, she stepped on the running board, then pulled herself onto the front seat. This beautiful sleigh would forever and ever remind her of Jack. Of his *maybe* offer to *sort of* try again and *hopefully...*

She bit her lip, vaguely aware of car lights on the road, then an engine, a door, and the thud of footsteps on the driveway.

Her heart tripped. Was Henry coming back? Did he have a gun? Was she in danger?

She ducked below the seat but sneaked her head out to look and see...

"Jack?" She popped up, stunned to see him hauling his suitcase.

He dropped the bag and walked directly toward the sleigh without saying a word.

"What are you doing here?"

She stared at him, her head spinning and her poor, poor heart racing in high gear.

Still silent, he hoisted himself up in one graceful move, took the seat next to her and put his cold bare hands on her cheeks.

"I'm not going."

She blinked at him.

"I'm not leaving you again," he said, his voice gravelly and emotional. "I'm not walking out on Christmas or ever. And I'm not hoping we can make this work in the spring."

She let out a whimper of disbelief.

"I am in love with you, Cindy Starling. I've missed ten years and I'm not missing another minute."

"But...Vermont...your mom..."

"I already told her I'm staying, and even at two in the morning on the East Coast, she cheered this decision. She said if I didn't come back to you before Christmas morning, she'd disown me. She told me the whole retirement home was rooting for us to get back together."

For some reason, that was the thing that brought tears to her eyes.

"This is where I belong, Cin. With you, with Nic, at Snowberry Lodge. Please, please let me stay, let me love you again, and let me be the man I know I can be. Start tonight. Now. On this sleigh, on this mountain, with me."

"Jack..."

"Just say yes."

"Yes." She barely whispered the word and his lips covered hers, warm and familiar. He kissed her with the same passion and promise as the first time. Only tonight, she knew this was forever.

CHRISTMAS MORNING DAWNS at Snowberry Lodge—but the season of love, laughter, and surprises is only just beginning. As snow drifts through the canyons and blankets the mountains in winter magic, hearts will be tested, new connections will spark, and family bonds will grow stronger than ever.

Nicole finds herself swept into a romance that changes her whole perspective about life. MJ's friendship with a mysterious guest stirs curiosity and concern. And Gracie hopes that her plans for Benny and his new puppy don't come back to bite her.

Don't miss Snowfall in Park City, the next book in the *Christmas in the Canyons* series—where every flurry brings another chance at holiday joy.

Christmas in the Canyons by Hope Holloway and Cecelia Scott

Sleigh Bells in Park City
Snowfall in Park City
Mistletoe in Park City
Midnight in Park City

LOOKING for another Christmas collaboration from Hope Holloway and Cecelia Scott? Enjoy a Carolina Christmas, a charming, heartwarming holiday series that will whisk you away to a dreamy winter in the Blue Ridge mountains.

Carolina Christmas by Hope Holloway and Cecelia Scott

The Asheville Christmas Cabin
The Asheville Christmas Gift
The Asheville Christmas Wedding
The Asheville Christmas Tradition

If you're in the mood to bask in the sunshine of a gorgeous beach, fall in love with an unforgettable cast of characters, and get lost in stories you cannot put down... you've come to the right authors!

Other family saga beach reads by
Hope Holloway and Cecelia Scott

Hope Holloway

Coconut Key
Shellseeker Beach
Seven Sisters

***

Cecelia Scott

Sweeney House
Young at Heart

***

Collaborations by Hope and Cecelia

Carolina Christmas
The Destin Diaries

***

Visit www.hopeholloway.com and www.ceceliascott.com
for details about all of their books!

About The Authors

Hope Holloway is the author of charming, heartwarming women's fiction featuring unforgettable families and friends, and the emotional challenges they conquer. After more than twenty years in marketing, she launched a new career as an author of beach reads and feel-good fiction. A mother of two adult children, Hope and her husband of thirty years live in Florida. When not writing, she can be found walking the beach with her two rescue dogs, who beg her to include animals in every book. Visit her site at www.hopeholloway.com.

Cecelia Scott is an author of light, bright women's fiction that explores family dynamics, heartfelt romance, and the emotional challenges that women face at all ages and stages of life. Her debut series, Sweeney House, is set on the shores of Cocoa Beach, where she lived for more than twenty years. Her books capture the salt, sand, and spectacular skies of the area and reflect her firm belief that life deserves a happy ending, with enough drama and surprises to keep it interesting. Cece currently resides in north Florida with her husband and beloved kitty. Visit her site at www.ceceliascott.com